EVENING OUT

Winner of the

FLANNERY O'CONNOR AWARD

FOR SHORT FICTION

Evening Out

Stories by David Walton

The University of Georgia Press
Athens

4/1983
am. Lit.

Copyright © 1983 by David Walton
Published by the University of Georgia Press
Athens, Georgia 30602

The paper in this book meets the guidelines
for permanence and durability of the Committee
on Production Guidelines for Book Longevity of
the Council on Library Resources.

Printed in the United States of America

Library of Congress Cataloging in Publication Data

Walton, David.
    Evening out.

    Contents: Evening out—Moogle boogled—
Synaphongenuphon—[etc.]
    I. Title.
PS3573.A4727E9 1982   813'.54   82-8398
ISBN 0-8203-0629-0   AACR2

Second printing

As I was on my way to St. Ives,
I met a man who had seven wives.
Each wife had seven cats,
And each cat seven kits.

How many were going to St. Ives?

—Old English Riddle

CONTENTS

EVENING OUT

EVENING OUT

I was at the typewriter, working on an examination of structural patterns in Huysmans' *Against the Grain*, when Carol Cole called.

"Come have dinner with us," she said.

It had been mild, unseasonably mild for January that afternoon, with temperatures in the sixties and lower seventies, the air balmy and clear. I'd gone shopping and for a walk in the park, and hadn't sat down to work until almost four, and by now had made it through only two of the four patterns I thought would be needed to fill out an article. This was my year to come up for tenure, and I wanted especially to be giving myself to my work just now.

And besides, I'd seen Carol and Larry just a couple of nights earlier, when I'd gone over to watch *The Many Loves of Charles II* on their color TV.

"I can't," I told her. "I thought I'd work through till I got hungry, and then just fix myself a sandwich or something. Besides, I thought Larry was in New Orleans."

"He gets in tonight. Bobette just went out to the airport to get him. That's part of the surprise," she told me.

"Surprise, what surprise?"

"Oh, now. It wouldn't be a surprise, would it, if I told you ahead of time?"

"Well—what about if I came over around nine?"

"Nine?"

"Eight-thirty, then, see, first I have to—"

"Make it seven-thirty," Carol said, and hung up the phone.

I soon found, contrary to any apprehensions I may have had, that the prospect of somewhere to go that evening speeded my work along, so that by the time I left the house, at a little past seven-thirty, it was with six more pages finished, and only another three or four to do when I got back.

It was still warm out, still with something of that buoyant, springtime feel to the air. Just the night before I'd

11

watched television clips of ice storms in Ohio and Michigan, trees completely covered with ice, power lines pulled down. But here people were out on their porches, cooking on hibachis, riding around with all the windows down—though with something of an edge, too, I was feeling, as if people recognized this was only a fluke, and likely to be gone momentarily. Driving over I kept noticing a tendency on people's part to rush the traffic signals, pull out the moment a light changed green, people kept crowding and racing you. Just recently Pennsylvania had gone over to a right turn on red policy, with the result of a general decay in street etiquette—the distinction between a right turn with caution after coming completely to a stop and a turn anyway whenever and however one cared to make it proving, like the one between flammable and inflammable, too subtle for the public mind to grasp. Several times driving over there I was almost clipped, and then people invariably would be indignant, honking their horns and shaking their fists at me, like they thought I was to blame.

The Coles lived on Mendel Street in the Company district, in what in Pittsburgh are known as two-window houses —narrow, high-peaked frame houses, former mill-owned houses, so named because they're only two windows wide. Recently this style of house and section of town had become fashionable, and the block gone over to a number of hip young architects and lawyers and similar early risers, who'd done it up in a panoply of mirror facades and pebble lawns and railroad-tie foliage beds, crammed with all sorts of exotic growths—an elegant devastation in which the Cole house stood out for simplicity and lack of pretension, and for having adhered to at least the basic outlines of the original design.

The first thing Larry and Carol had done when they bought their house was to gut it completely, pull out all the old plaster and wiring and plumbing, and set out to build it over from the inside out. They lived in the house while they did the work, and anything they didn't know how to do, they learned as they came to.

It was Carol I'd known originally—Carol had been a student of mine two or three years back—and they became friends really only after they'd bought the house. I helped them tear the plaster out, and after that took to stopping by more or less regularly, in the evenings sometimes if there was something good on TV, and for Sunday brunch. They were good, uncomplex people, people for whom disaster was a clogged storm drain or an exorbitant estimate, a new shower nozzle or a completed duct layout cause for party and celebration.

In the summers I kept a little salad garden in the back, and some of my most pleasant memories of the three summers past are of that hour at the end of the day, greeting them as they came in from work, sitting out on the porch roof with the plants, sipping iced tea and exchanging pleasantries with passersby, and watching the sun slip behind the tree-tops at the end of the block.

Bobette, incidentally, is a mutual friend of the Coles, a former nun, a painter (it is Bobette whose works are so conspicuously stored about the walls of the Cole house), most recently a carpenter and motorcycle enthusiast, who headquarters in Pittsburgh, but is rarely here oftener than three or four days a month.

Carol was lighting the candles on the dinner table when I pulled up outside. One of the novel features of the Cole house is that the living and dining areas are on the second floor, fronted by high, undraped windows, giving an impression of casual openness to the street, while the sleeping and private quarters are downstairs, sheltered behind lilacs and firethorn, trellises of yellow trumpet and clematis, and what appear to be, on a closer inspection turn out to be, three large, weatherbeaten wooden packing crates.

Carol waved, and came down the stairs to meet me. The front door was paneled stained glass, and through it I could follow her descent, fractured, elongated, shape taking form only as she arrived at the door. Carol Cole is an exceptionally tall woman, and generally dresses to accentuate her height, tonight in a peach-colored drape, off the shoulder and slit above the knee.

"Charl"—stretching hands out to greet me.

Recently I'd been thinking Carol was in something of a slump, the sign of that being that her voice, never too hale to begin with, had been sinking lower, and breathier, until half the time anymore even the repetition was too whispery to bother asking her to repeat.

But tonight she was glowing, hands, eyes, the ends of her hair crackling with excited energy.

"Are Larry and Bobette back yet?"

"They should be here any minute now. Larry's plane got detoured around Nashville, can you imagine? They're having blizzards in Nashville."

Another distinctive feature of the Cole house is that after a narrow entry and stairway, the whole second floor is open, eating, cooking, living areas all one single continuous area—though you quickly come to realize how subtly each space is individualized and defined—giving you, as you crest the stairs, the impression of coming into the whole house at once.

Tonight the whole area was candlelit, the table, on top of the television and refrigerator, a candle on the open door of the oven, napkins blooming out of carved napkin rings, half a dozen carnation heads floating in a bowl of water in the center of the table.

"What's all this?"

She could contain herself no longer. From behind her back she thrust into my hands the rolled up magazine section of the Sunday newspaper, saying, "Take a look at page 78."

I turned to page 78, and here I suppose is an example of

deferred cognition, because I must have stared a full minute at that page without identifying those stairs as the ones I'd just come up, that room as the one I was standing in.

I glanced over to Carol, who was beaming expectantly.

"What is it?"

"It doesn't come out until Sunday. They sent an advance copy over for us to see. The photographers were here in October but we weren't saying anything to anyone for fear they might not print it after all."

Then I recognized Larry's mother in one of the pictures.

"This is your place." I had to say it over two or three more times, "This is your house."

There were three and a half pages of photographs, two of them in full color, shots of the front and back and each interior area, and even one down on the garden plot from one of the second-story windows.

It was an innovative plot in its way, a series of five overlapping terraces, each one bordered by a row of blue insulator caps I'd rescued from the phone company dump two summers before.

"Has Larry seen this?"

"It just came this afternoon. Bobette's seen it, Bobette was here when the mail came. We're not saying anything to Larry till he gets here."

"Look how many of Bobette's paintings show up in the photographs," I said.

"Eighteen in all. Though you know they did leave out the one across from the bed, which she and I both feel is her best by far."

The text focused on the individualistic features of the house; it was a useful, literate text, going beyond mere surface attractiveness to point up the compactness and convenience of the design.

" 'Personal as a portrait,' " I read.

Carol gave a deprecatory shrug.

"Oh, well, what d'you expect, after all it is only the

Sunday supplement."

Ten minutes later, when Larry and Bobette came in the door, Carol was at the sinkboard stirring up a green concoction, and I was on the couch leafing through the Sunday paper. Larry came up first—big, bounding, burly, redheaded, shaggy red beard, six feet four and weighing nearly 250 pounds.

"I've got news, I've got news!"

Carol offered him a cheek and said, "Before you start, just let me finish here."

Like a pinball he was across the room to me.

"Chuck, say, Chuck, you remember those bins—"

"Say, Lar," I said, handing him the folded-open magazine section, "here's something might interest you."

"—wallpaper bins I designed last October," giving the page a cursory glance, "well, I don't know whether I told you this before or not but *saaay!*"

Bobette appeared at the top of the stairs, lugging a squat cardboard box with airholes bored around the sides, like a mail order of baby chicks. Since turning to carpentry, Bobette has adopted a kind of coveralls chic—this evening a pair of stained but very immaculate white alls over a violet clenched-fist T-shirt, with matching violet laces in her clogs. Bobette is short and somewhat squarish, about twenty-five, twenty-six—though not so short, maybe, as just short in comparison to the rest of us, all of us—Carol Cole, who is six feet even, included—six feet or over. In reality I don't suppose she would be anything less than five-four or five-three.

"Watch, it's dripping."

"Set it over here." Carol pointed to a spot on the floor by the sink where newspaper had been laid out. Bobette took a penknife out of one of her coveralls pockets and started cutting the twine.

"What is it?" I asked.

"Oysters." Carol lifted the lid and motioned for me to come see—piles and piles of oysters, nesting in a bed of

16

cracked ice. "Eleven dozen oysters. Larry brought them home from New Orleans with him."

"Hey," said Larry on the mention of his name, "this is our house."

"See," I told Carol, "it was the same with me, it took a couple of minutes before I could recognize it."

"We were remarking on the same thing this afternoon," Carol said, "we figure it's at least forty-five seconds."

She reached into the refrigerator and brought out a bottle of wine in a bucket and towel, which she and Larry danced across the floor, and Bobette took a corkscrew out of her coveralls and opened it, and we cranked open the front windows and threw bits of cracked ice down at passersby, and Carol got out a joint of the dope her sister had brought home from Honduras in a Tampax last summer, and I spilt wine on the floor and Larry slipped in it, and the four of us ended up under the sinkboard, shoving and laughing like imbeciles.

"Eleven—"

"—dozen—"

"—oysters."

"And the best part is," Larry said, "for as much as it costs you down there, it would pay us, a group of us, every month or so, to chip in and send somebody down there."

Bobette got a couple of grip tools and pairs of work gloves out of her coveralls, and showed me how to open the shells. Four big oval trays had been set out on the sinkboard, and Carol lined these with rock salt, laid the oysters out on them, and spread them with the green concoction she'd been mixing up when Larry and Bobette came in the door, while Bobette related to us the story of a cat her uncle had owned, that was so freaked by the oysters being opened that he clawed all the way up to the top of the wall.

"Why rock salt?" I wanted to know.

"It keeps them from tipping over in the oven," Carol said.

17

"No," Bobette thought, "it retains the heat and keeps them warm after they come out."

Three dozen more were put aside to be eaten raw, with a white and a red sauce that Carol was mixing up, and Larry stirred up a batter for frying the rest. The Oysters Rockefeller took only five minutes in the oven, and with them from the oven came two pans of tomato muffins, and from the refrigerator a big salad blanketed with wedges of avocado and bits of *feta* cheese, and Larry's fried oysters were draining on paper towel, and in no time at all it seemed we were seated at the table, surrounded by trays and trays of oysters.

"Mm."

"Mm."

"Mm."

Larry said, "I was down there three days, and all I did was eat. I had oysters for breakfast and oysters for lunch, I had oysters three times a day, and I could get up tomorrow morning and eat oysters three more times a day."

"Mmm."

"Mmm."

"Mmm."

After a few minutes Carol came around with a tray and collected shells, and Larry and Bobette brought around trays of the oysters raw and Oysters Rockefeller, and we all loaded up again. The tomato muffins were burned a little on the bottom, the way I like them, and in with the fried oysters were little starflakes of fried batter that nobody else wanted but me.

"Mmmm."

"Mmmm."

"Mmmm."

Every couple of minutes Larry would get up and go find some new feature in the article to call to our attention.

"You know what this means," he said—"do you ever think this way, that what happens to you doesn't just happen to you, but's part of a whole group push, however unwitting

18

the initial effort might have been given. This doesn't just happen to us, to Carol and me, but it's you, and Bobette, it's all the people we're closest to."

"What was your news?" I asked.

"News? Omigosh—you know I nearly forgot. Chuck. You remember those bins I designed, those wallpaper bins in October for those people in Cincinnati?"

"Sure, I remember."

"Well, I don't know whether I told you this before or not, but when I went down there, to New Orleans, one of my reasons for going down there was to meet these people who wanted to take a look at my designs."

"You told me you were—"

"Well. I don't know whether I told you this part of it or not, but these people, who I was meeting with, are distributors for wallpaper for the whole south and southwestern part of the United States."

"Larry!"

"And there's a chance now—"

"Larry!"

"Just a chance now—"

"Larry, that's wonderful!"

"Larry, that's great!"

We all got up and hugged Larry and shook his hand. Bobette opened another bottle of wine, and Carol proposed a toast, a more solemn toast this time, "To sprezzatura. No more angst or ennui. No more wry ironies or glum understatements. From now on, all will be sprezzatura."

A quieter mood came over the table now. My own feeling, as much as anything else at that moment, was one of wonder and surprise; for much as I like and respect Larry Cole, he's always been someone I've admired more for personal than for professional qualities. While I've always felt sure he was a fine enough architect, he always seemed to me too compliant—too quick to accommodate—to ever be anything of a serious success; the kind of man who, if you'd come to visit him, would not only walk you out to the door, and out onto the porch, and down the walk to your car, and hold the car door open for you while you were getting inside, but, finding the hinges on the door stiff, as he did with me on one occasion, would go back in for an oil can and oil them for you. For him now to have a success seemed not merely an individual achievement, it seemed the affirmation of a whole life principle.

"It's all coming together," he told us, "this," slapping the rolled-up magazine section into his hands, "now this, all the pieces are finally fitting in."

Carol brought around the last half tray of raw oysters, and there was a little to-do about who would take the last several. Bobette found a nascent pearl in one of hers, and told again the story of the cat that clawed all the way to the top of the wall, and then for a few minutes nobody said anything, each of us occupied with his own corner of napkin or handle of butter knife. Carol brought around a basket of kumquats, which Larry had also brought back from New Orleans with him, and which I'd never eaten before. It seemed strange to eat a citrus peel and all; Bobette, I noticed, didn't even bother spitting the seeds out of hers.

"Who's for coffee?" Carol said, setting around saucers and cups.

I excused myself and got up from the table.

The second-floor powder room is one of the few flaws of execution in the Cole house, a narrow, cramped, triangular space tucked underneath the stairway to the loft, with the backs of the washing machine and hot-water heater enclosures intruding onto your legs—so that you have to list to leak, so to speak. But tonight even standing irritations were absorbed into the general glow. I think I mentioned earlier that this was my year to come up for tenure. These ceremonial ascenduals, I was finding, are a poisoned chalice borne to the lips of victor and vanquished alike. I know of one man, his case narrowly defeated in review committee after review committee, who retreated into his basement to play with electric trains; another who, sailing easily through every one, began shedding latencies—wife, children, house, car, finishing the year out with a sixteen-year-old nephew, living in a camper van he parked each night outside a different one of his senior faculty's homes. One tells himself at these times that he won't allow what is after all only a ritual and arbitrary process to impinge upon his mind, but still the signs had been beginning to tell, not in any large or very recognizable way maybe, but in various small, inconspicuous ways, ways that probably only I was cognizant of.

But tonight, almost for the first time, I began to allow myself to think as Larry had said, that success could be contagious, the success of one sparking the success of another —of things I might do and places I could go, things I'd been saving up until now, I could see Europe, I could take up horseback riding—

These pleasing reveries were interrupted by the sound of a crash, followed quickly by another, and then another in the other room. I hurried out to find Carol having flung three, and about to fling the fourth of a lime parfait against the wall.

My first quick impression, however, as I came into the room, was that whatever this was, Bobette was in some way responsible. It wasn't anything particular, nothing you could put your finger on, more some gesture or expression, some quality of participation you might have expected to be there but wasn't—like one of these oriental things that exists only in the absence of itself. Bobette was sitting by the windows, half around in her chair with her hand up beside her face, as if shielding herself—as if in chagrin, my thought was.

I have to say, though, that for me Bobette has always been something of an unsettling presence. When Bobette went into the nunnery, she took the feminization of her older brother's name—a point I think speaks volumes in itself—and kept a diminutive of the name after she came out

21

again two years later. While in the nunnery, Bobette spent most of her time organizing the nuns into a democratic cell. The order has since been disbanded. At present she's suing the Benevolent Brotherhood of Trade Carpenters for discriminatory practices in its apprenticeship program—all activities Bobette speaks of with some accomplishment and pride, as no doubt she ought. In her own mind, I think, Bobette is the selfless crusader, flinging herself heedless of the cost against the barricades of entrenched privilege. But for me she shows signs of a dangerously contentious personality.

Even her paintings are disturbing, dark, swirling, unstrained masses. For a long time she was painting the backs of things—backs of buses, the backs of rundown garages, rear views of people's conversations. Lately she's started a new series, painting corners and eaves of buildings—a whole neighborhood of paintings of eaves and gables.

I have to confess, too, to a personal note here: that for the past three or four times we've been together, Bobette has been dropping off to sleep, just dozing off, one time right at the dinner table. I hadn't thought much about it until Carol Cole told me that it happened only on times I was there.

Carol tossed the last of the parfait dishes, glass shattering, green shoots streaking out across the wall.

"Runaway kitchens," she was saying, "take-it-easy kitchens. Laminates. Patinas. Defining without dividing. Though fine enough I'd suppose for crooked cocks"—this last one directed apparently at me.

Larry was standing just inside the kitchen area, watching with what might have been dulled amazement, or else a bemused compliance.

"What's going on here?" I said.

Carol began heaving the trivets at the wall.

"She gets like this," he told me.

"Gets like this? What're you talking about? She's breaking things."

"Yeah, well," he conceded, "she is a little more violent

this time than usual. But I've been seeing this coming for a couple of months now. Just leave her go, she comes out of it eventually."

With one long sweep of her arm Carol sent cups, dishes, the bowl of carnations flying, water, wine, hot wax sloshing across the floorboards. What made it so strange was that it was so deliberate, so cool—offhanded, almost.

"Carol," I said. She'd picked up the carafe and was about to fling it after the trivets and parfait glasses. I took hold of her arm and said, "Carol. Don't you think it's time you stopped this now?"

She turned, coming fast around, the anger right to the surface. This was showing me a different side.

"Well? Aren't you going to say what a triumph?"

"What's this now?"

"Isn't that what you always say, ooo," in a mocking parody of my own mannerly style, "French onion soup, ooo, what a triumph. Ooo, pumpkin bread, what a triumph! Say, don't we need a prescription for this coffee?"

I backed off a little from this, and over my shoulder Larry said, "See, you try to interfere, it just aggravates her. You have to just leave her go, she'll run herself down sooner or later."

Carol, meanwhile, had grabbed up one of the jar lamps and was lashing it, down now to the cord and a chunk of base, against the tabletop, the dividers, the backs of the stow-away chairs. When she moved in on the hanging desk, though, that I'd been the one to spot at the Etna flea mart the last October, I felt I had to intervene.

"Carol. I'm not going to stand here and watch this. If you're going on with this, I'm leaving."

"Well." Again, with unnerving quickness, she was on me, a turn so graceful and automatic, so totally reflexive, it was doubly unnerving—an eerie, icy poise.

"Go on. I'm surprised you even stayed this long. Usually it's not half an hour you're not squirming in your seat complaining how much work you have to do at home. Well. Go on."

She pointed to the stairway.

"What're you waiting for?"

There was nothing to do then but to wait it out. I went over by the windows and took a seat next to the amaryllis, near where Bobette was sitting—slipping unconsciously into something of Bobette's same pose, turned half around, my hand at my temple.

Carol had taken up the fireplace poker now, and was going around striking it against the Dorcas panels, the strips of mirror glass that separated the panels, hard down on the epoxy guard underneath the freestanding fireplace, all, I noted, for whatever observational interest it might have, features that she herself had worked the hardest on.

"Like the Utts," she was saying, "people you haven't heard from since high school, seen in years, not to mention your friends, which would be fine enough, except it can never be these casual massings, oh, no, one or two of those, it always has to be these candlelit cantatas, never more than five six at a time—"

I had to admit, though, to a kind of logic to all this. It was only, I was thinking, what had been implicit in the situation all along. It was all those evening-long discussions of where the stairway should go and what color the exposed pipes should be painted and three trips a week out to Busy Beaver and Carol never quite so enthralled and Larry never quite noticing and sleeping on a mattress on the floor for three years and a lot more I suppose besides—though I try to make a point of not burdening my relationships with too many gratuitous insights.

The poker left scooped indentations in the wall that the candlelight reflected on like yellow petals on water, an effect not wholly unappealing in itself. I sat staring out the window at the Wednesday night meeting of the Alcoholics Anonymous in one of the second-floor rooms of the Episcopal

Church across the street, watching one of their number test-
ify, while they in turn were beginning to come around in
their chairs to watch us.

"Even sitting here"—she'd more or less finished with the
walls now, and was starting on the tabletop—"it drains me,
the energy out of me, just knowing what's gone into every
piece, what's done, and to be done—though all of you, I suppose, with your prospects, and your prospectuses, and all
your pros-sess-sees—"

I was willing to let it go that far, but when she started
for the sinkboard, which for me is one of the sacred objects
in that house, a seven-foot slab of driftwood that had had to
have its own trailer to bring it back from Cape May two summers before, and three sets of arms thirty-eight consecutive
Wednesday evenings, through thirty-eight episodes of *The
Plantaganets*, oiling and rubbing it—

"Now just a minute here—"

At that same moment Carol was passing underneath the
secret lair, the recessed ceiling duct in which the two Cole
cats, Tristram (whom they called Dristan) and Other would
wait a whole evening out sometimes for somebody to pass
underneath, so they could leap yolping and screeching onto
his neck. This was a habit they'd picked up in the early days
of the Cole house, when there were a thousand open aper-
tures and slots out of which a cat could stalk the unwary
guest. Most of the regulars to the house knew by now to
detour the spot, but invariably in the course of any evening
there would be one person who forgot, with the result, as
now, of all action being halted for a five-count—

"Oh!"

I ought to mention, too, that through all this she had
looked quite beautiful, hair raging, eyes flashing, a wild, fluid
energy.

"Oh, Larry!"

The table was overturned, tablecloth twisted into a snarl
amid broken china and glass, smashed lamps and chairs, a

green, viscous ooze, like some sort of vegetable secretion, trickling down the walls.

"Oh, my!"

Larry went over and put his arms around her and hugged her, saying, "Now, honey, now." Over her shoulder he said to me, "See, you just leave her go, sooner or later she works out of it on her own."

He gave her a little nudge and squeeze, making a joke of it, "Hey, got a little flipped over there, didn't we, pancake?"

"Hey," I said, picking up my cue, "how about that, hey."

"Oh, my, oh, Larry, oh, no"—Carol looked around the room in growing dismay—"we've got to get this cleaned up."

She began tugging at the tablecloth, trying to free it from the debris, while at the same time right an overturned piano stool.

"Hey."

"Hon."

"Car-ol."

With the end of the tablecloth she tried wiping up the dribbles of parfait before they could reach the baseboard.

"Aw, honey, now come on, leave that be, we don't have to be doing that now."

"You don't understand, I called your Mom and Dad, tomorrow your Mom and Dad are coming over, I called them about the article and they're coming over for lunch, oh, Larry, I couldn't let them see the place like this."

"Hey, now, they wouldn't—"

"Look," I said, "there's plenty of time tomorrow morning for that. Why don't we sit down now. Have a cup of coffee. Maybe another glass of wine—"

"Glass of wine?" She turned to me incredulous. "Cup of coffee? You want me to sit down and have a cup of coffee?"

For a moment it looked as though she was about to start up again. But then Bobette said:

"Why don't we go up to Just Desserts and have short-

26

cake."

It was the first she'd spoken, and her words, for maybe that reason, had something of a salutary effect.

"We were going to have dessert anyway. Well, why don't we go up and have shortcake, and then decide about this when we get back."

In our eagerness to be out the door we didn't bother with coats or sweaters, and indeed, there was little need. Outside was as balmy as a springtime evening, the sky clear, a few high, fleecy clouds cutting across the sickle of a quarter-moon—though still with something of that rangy feel I'd noticed earlier in the air, a little more ragged, a little uncertain maybe now. All up the block there were cars with their wheels parked up on the curb, and in the houses we went by the sounds of arguments, and telephones ringing unanswered.

Bobette and I took the lead, Larry and Carol coming up a little behind. By the time we reached the corner, I noticed they were beginning to lag behind, and at the next corner when we looked back, they'd stopped, about half a block back of us, and were standing deep in conversation.

"What should we do," I asked Bobette, "should we wait on them?"

Bobette shrugged noncommittally.

After a minute, Larry came jogging up the street to join us.

"Ah—Chuck. Bobette. Bobette, I wonder if I could have Chuck alone maybe for a minute?"

Bobette shrugged noncommittally.

Larry has a habit, though, anytime he's trying not to offend someone, of making so scrupulous an attempt not to offend that he has inevitably that very result.

"It'll just take a minute," he kept assuring her.

"All right, it's all right"—Bobette practically stomping her foot.

Larry put his arm around my shoulder and led me off a little ways. "Ah—Chuck. Chuck, ah, listen, I don't know whether I've told you this before or not—"

"Listen, Larry, now don't go feeling you have to—"

"—a marriage counselor."

"A marriage counselor?"

"For two months now. Partly it's been the house. When we had the house we didn't have so much time for other things, but lately, now that most of that's done with—well, I don't know whether I've told you this before—"

"You know, Lar, you don't—"

"—is inverted."

"Inverted."

"Partly it's the shaft doesn't have enough skin to cover, is a lot of the problem, and part of it I guess has to do with the way the sacs fill up, but what it comes down to is that when I go up, really I go down."

"No," I said, "you hadn't told me that."

"Circumcision would alleviate some of the problem, I suppose, but what it really means is for both of us to get satisfaction, she has to lie off the side of the bed with her face to the floor, which Carol tends to feel is a degrading position."

"Oh, I can understand," I said.

"Though there are women," Larry hurried to tell me, "and you can take my word for it, that don't see it that way, that in fact prefer it that way."

"Oh, I can imagine, I can imagine," I said.

We were pacing a circuit roughly equidistant between where Bobette and where Carol were standing. Larry's arm was across my back, his fingers working my shoulder, a movement totally unconscious, I'm sure, but the more disconcerting for being that. I've always had a strong sense of Larry's presence, his strong physical presence. A part of that I know has to do with my sister's being a redhead—although I feel I've pretty much worked through that part of it now.

"So, Chuck, I was wondering—"

"Listen, Lar, why don't Bobette and I—"

At the same time he was reaching for his wallet, but I waved that gesture aside.

"Bobette and I'll go on and have our shortcake, then maybe after that we can stop back, or we'll all see each other another night."

"Listen, maybe tomorrow I could—"

"Tomorrow you'll call me," I said, "and we'll talk it all through. Now you go worry about Carol, and let Bobette and me take care of ourselves."

Larry hurried back to Carol with this solution, and I walked back up to explain the situation to Bobette—a task more onerous than I might have anticipated. I tried giving only the bare outlines, without going into any detail—which Bobette took for evasiveness. She began eyeing me with increasing skepticism and disdain.

"All right, that's all right," she started saying, in the same tone I'd heard her use on Larry a few minutes earlier.

"Of course now if you'd rather—"

"No, no, that's all right. We were going to have our dessert anyway, so let's have our dessert."

We walked most of the rest of the way in silence.

Just Desserts lay at the end of the next block, the main block of the Company Strip, in the reconstructed tipple of the old Shaler mills, one of the city's pre-Carnegiean companies that gave the district its name. Two of the long mill sheds had been converted into indoor malls, retaining the corrugated roofs and the window strips along the top of the walls, the end panels painted with scenes of local industry— the open hearth—the air brake—the romance of the river trade.

In the front was a bakeshop, in back, underneath the octagonal cone, a restaurant area, its walls lined with giant cooler cases, and inside, behind jagged mountain ranges of condensation, napoleons, eclairs, eighteen different varieties of shortcake glowing in a fluorescent hush.

As we were deliberating the menu, I noticed Bobette

picking at her napkin, arranging and rearranging it in her lap.

"How've you been, Bobette?" I said, thinking to put her at her ease. "Haven't seen too much of you lately."

She said, "You know, I'm always doing that. I had this stretch, December, in November, right before Christmas, where I was taking everything apart, lamps. All my lamps apart. My clocks apart. Getting down to the essences of things. I did it with words, too. Schopenhauer. Shopping for something higher. Hitler. Hit the liar. Hegel. He jelled. I'd get a letter, I'd have to take it apart on all the seams before I could take it out of the envelope and read it."

"I do that, too," I said, "open my envelopes on all the seams. And milk cartons. Before I can take out my trash, I have to take all the milk cartons apart and flatten them out."

"You do that, I do that, too," Bobette said.

"Isn't it strange," I said, "how many of the things that are peculiar to ourselves, other people imagine are peculiar only to them."

Bobette laughed a little over that, and I had a pleasing sense of a bad moment having been gotten nicely by. After our orders came, though, as we were starting in to eat, I noticed Bobette tearing little bits off her napkin, rolling them between her fingers and slipping them under the match pack in the ashtray.

"Is something bothering you, Bobette?" I finally said.

"No, no."

"Is it me? Something I said?"

"It's nothing, no."

"Or something I've done?" I feel I must be doing something to make you so uneasy."

"It's, no, I don't want you thinking that. It's one of my little quirks, I have a thousand of these little quirks. It's just this place, anytime I come here, I always have this feeling I'm going to go flying out of my chair."

Above our heads loomed the tipple shell, painted fuchsia blue on the inside and hung with an ascending series of mobiles, bits of metallic silver flashing and vanishing in the gloom, the gradation of these, or some device of the lighting giving these a false perspective, a feeling of infinite rising; I'd noticed it, too. Like the whole room was going suddenly to turn over on you. The tables were cramped, too close together, the waitresses having to go up on tiptoes to pass between.

"And you know they left the shaft open under here, I know, I know, it's only phobic, but still it's that idea, of all that space down there under you."

"Why do you come here, then?"

Bobette shrugged. "You know, I hate to say anything. It's where people like to go. It's like always having to have the aisle seat."

We'd pushed our plates away, and more or less pushed back from the table. Her features, which I'd thought previously of as being stubby, were more precisely squarish, her face angled off, or rather, too much rounded off, too symmetrical. Her fingers were short and blunt, though well shaped and well tended, and remarkably clean for a woman who was both a painter and a carpenter.

"We could just leave, you know."

"No, I don't want to do that. I think these are the very impulses you ought to control. You give in to these, and you're only undermining your whole discipline and make yourself weak in general."

"And meantime," I said, "I'm sitting here to please you, and these other people, no doubt, out of deference to ourselves probably, are remaining in their seats, instead of climbing up onto them and raving like they'd no doubt like to do"—at the same time rising from my chair, motioning the waitress for our check. Bobette hesitated a moment, but just a moment—and then the smile, abrupt, and a little surprised at itself, like I'd never seen from her before.

Then as we were leaving there was a moment where she reached to take the check and without thinking I handed it over, and was rewarded with a second of those smiles—having passed, I could see, some particular test, met some private criteria.

"Oh."

"My."

"Those dishes, did you—"

"In the back?"

"Uff!"

"Chuck—Chuck. Do you remember a time back in November we were both at the Cole house and I said to you I was driving to Rochester the next day, do you remember that?"

"I remember you saying you were going to Rochester but you might drive to Youngstown first."

"And you looked at me. I said I had to drop packages off at my grandmother's because it might be too late to mail them, and you gave me this look, do you remember that?"

"I remember you saying you might drive to Youngstown, but I don't remember thinking anything about it, no."

"You didn't say to yourself I maybe might not be really going to do it?"

"I thought you were taking a trip, you're always taking trips, I wouldn't have thought any more about it."

"Well, there, you see, now that's another thing. I'm always doing that. Extrapolating from what I think people are thinking to what they're really thinking, when half the time probably they're not even thinking that much about me at all."

"Oh, well, now, I wouldn't know about that, but I know what you mean. I'm that way, too."

"Oh, not like me, I'm terrible that way."

"Oh, I don't know. I think I have a whole shadow career going for me for the evenings, where I sit around and brood out all the things that haven't really happened during the day."

We'd come to the light at Blevett and Nott, which,

just as we reached it, changed, and we were able to cross without missing a step, and I was thinking that this was the thing about Bobette, that Bobette was always putting obstacles up in front of herself, and what she appreciated in people was for somebody to go along ahead of her and clear them out of the way; and that now that I thought about it, that this was something I'd recognized earlier about Bobette, when I'd first met her, but let slip my mind in the meantime.

"—like a maraschino cherry," she was saying, "that two swallows later you've forgotten you've even had. Like this afternoon, I must have spent three hours at my bench this afternoon making up lists of sevens—things that go into sevens. Like the seven dwarfs. Seven deadly sins. The seven warning signals of cancer."

"The seven cardinal virtues, Bobette, this is remarkable—"

"The seven wonders of the world. There's more than you might think. The seven sister colleges. The seven against Thebes."

"Bobette, this is truly remarkable, because this very afternoon in my office—"

"The seven grades in the Cecchetti Council of America System of Ballet."

"The seven veils in the Dance of the Seven Veils, Bobette—"

"Do you like plastic things?"

"Plastic things?"

As we came round the corner onto Mendel I noticed that the pavement was wet, but figured somebody had been out washing a car or hosing down the sidewalk.

"You mean like clear plastic like—"

Suddenly from behind the bushes five or six, maybe as many as eight small boys leapt out with buckets of water and fistfuls of mud, doused and pelted us, and raced away squealing, buckets clattering back around the buildings.

"*Guhhh!*"

33

"Don't—"

"Bobette?"

"Here, just let me—"

We were a sorry sight, drenched head to foot and splashed with mud, faces covered with mud, all down the front of Bobette's clean coveralls splattered. She made an attempt to wipe them off, and then gave up and started laughing. We both started laughing. There wasn't much more you could do.

Larry Cole came hurrying up the street, "Those—kids, those—Turrell kids, those are those same goldsmith's kids—"

He shepherded us down to the side of the house and started the hose over us.

"I was trying to watch for you, they've been out here the last hour catching people, those are those same dagblame goldsmith's kids pulled the green tomatoes off the vines last summer."

"Larry," Carol called down from one of the upstairs windows, "bring them in here."

"Get the worst of it off out here," Larry said, "fix you up with something warm once we get you inside."

"It's only water," we both said, "no, really, this'll do fine."

But the air was chill that hit us now, and I could see Bobette beginning to shiver. The mud had gotten all in her hair, and would have to be shampooed out.

"Larry," Carol called down, "get them *in* here, it's *cold* out there."

"I'm getting the worst of it out here. Bring them down some towels that we can wrap them in. She and I still have some pretty heavy talking over to do," he told us, "but I think we're beginning to come to an understanding of sorts."

Carol met us at the door with blankets and a stack of dry towels. Behind her, through the open door to the bedroom, I could see a fire blazing, a little table laid out with teapot and mugs.

"There."

"Get you out of these."

As I was pulling off my trousers, I lost balance, and had a glimpse over my shoulder of bare breast and back, an embarrassing moment here, Bobette hurriedly pulling on a robe, and I turned quickly back around. Outside I'd felt—I couldn't say what now.

And plastic things? What was that supposed to mean?

"Here."

"Yourself down here where it's warm."

Carol shook blankets out over us, and Larry propped a couple pillows behind my back. Bobette had gone into the bathroom to rinse out her hair, and through the half-open door I could see an archway of blue, her elbow in a blue bathrobe each time she stepped back against the mirror on the inside of the door.

Larry began rubbing my feet with a towel, hard till they stung and burned.

"Ow! Wow! Hey!"

Carol reached back to pull the diaphanous violet drapes that enclosed the cushioned oval in front of the hearth into the Coles' much-alluded-to "womb tomb." The dousing, the cold plunge with the hose, and now the steady radiance of the fire soothed and yet had sensitized my skin to each fine detail, the texture of the pillow rubbing my ear, a foot, Larry's, jostling me underneath the covers.

Carol said, "I can see now where I can't always be making Larry make all the decisions and then not be satisfied when things aren't turning out the way I expect them."

And Larry said, "And I see where I can't always be letting the house occupy all our energy and time."

"Our whole lives, really."

"That's going to change now. We're going to let our lives spread out now, accept new responsibilities. Make our house a place to live in."

"Not let it dominate us completely."

35

"We're not even putting back what's happened here tonight."

"A few necessary repairs."

"Like the sink."

"The sink we'll have to take care of. And the table and chairs."

"But other than that—"

"Well, we're just going to have to wait and see. Bobette—"

"Bobette, could you get that light?"

Bobette was coming out of the bathroom, wrapped up in one of Carol's oversize bathrobes, a towel wrapped around her head, one hand clutching her throat while the other one swept the hem out of the way of her feet.

"The other one, too."

I'd pushed up onto one elbow to get a look at her face, but it was too far, as she bent to switch out the lamp, her face coming up against the shade as if to blow it out, the glare of the bulb bleached out her features, casting triplicate shadows onto the ceiling and the two corner angles behind her—"It's the limit," she was saying, and it was a second or two before I realized it was me she was speaking to, "of our ability to distinguish degrees of saliance, levels of loudness. Seven items is the limit of our span of immediate memory. All learning is divided into seven, the quadrivium—"

The drape caught on a snag, and as Carol reached back to give it a tug, as Bobette was squeezing in between us, I heard a tapping at the window, and turning my head saw the first streaks of rain, half congealed into snow—of Michigan's icestorm, starting against the glass.

MOOGLE BOOGLED

On alternate Tuesdays Leonard Parchman's wife Geraldine had her contact improvisation class, and those nights usually, if the weather was nice, Leonard got off the bus at the lower end of Forbes and walked the rest of the way home, past the university and hospitals, a slow swing around the Carnegie Institute grounds. Leonard was a lawyer working for the city in child abuse cases, and in a deliberate way reserved this first hour or so after work for emptying out and clearing away, the protective barrier he maintained between the Leonard of the evening and the Leonard of the day.

It was a mild, balmy evening, the fourth day of April and still a little ahead of the season. He sat for a while on one of the stone benches beside the Stephen Foster Memorial, watching the clouds and the promenaders, and then around six doubled back to Chancery Street to Fred's Franks.

He and Geraldine ate wholesome foods, thick lentil stews and zucchini breads they made together on Sunday evenings and ate the whole week through, so that on these evenings he rewarded himself with whatever sort of greedy concoction he could devise, tonight a footlong piled high with catsup, mustard, and onion, and a special cucumber relish they kept in a jar next to the cash register, fries, a strawberry triple shake. He loved the way the bun turned spongy in his hands, and big splots of filling dribbled down onto the napkin with every bite. Leonard's was the ethic of continuance through controlled deviation. He needn't do the things he did. He didn't have to live the life he did. It was a question of choice.

As he was opening his mouth to take another bite, a man about his own age—thirty, and looking vaguely familiar—came up and swung a mock fist into his arm, saying, "Len, hi, hey, how you been treating yourself?"

He looked—somebody he'd known in law school, maybe—much like Leonard himself, stocky build, shaggy hair, bushy, somewhat unkempt moustache, a wide tie pulled open at his neck.

"Say."

"Your own self."

"Fine, you been?"

"Steel Building. You know US Steel owns but doesn't occupy its whole building. I rent out space, edit the building newsletter. Features, interviews, some really way out stuff. I'll mail you a copy."

"Say."

"And say, you know who else's down there, Corrine Greenfield-Gillespie-before-she-got-married."

"Say, how is old Corrine?"

"She's working for Rockwell. I see her on the escalator every now and again."

Leonard still couldn't place him. He tried several names out on him, Dan Booth and Howard Barnett, both of which struck remarks, and he knew Geraldine apparently, but in his haste to dodge him it wasn't until he was halfway down the block he realized that this was Nick, Nick the Silversmith, who'd lived in Gina Armburster's basement the summer Gina Armburster decided that if she was going to divorce Clifford she was going to have to give up Gus Blodgett as well, who Gus tried to kill one night with a piece out of the Rickety sculpture, the summer of the great Pyrinate scare, three, four summers ago, the summer he fell off the tank monument in North Park and broke his arm. The summer he met Geraldine.

The thought of all this put him in mind to stop and see Gus, who lived on Meyran only a couple of blocks from here. Gus Blodgett was somebody Geraldine considered sleazy, and Leonard saw anymore only on nights like this when she was otherwise occupied, or he had dope to buy.

"Sit out here, think?"

Gus lived above a cleaners, and had a little side porch off the front room that you climbed out onto over the back of the couch and through one of the front windows. He pulled a joint the size of an index finger out of his shirt pocket and pointed it at Leonard.

"Doobie, mon?"

"Ha-ho, doobie," Leonard laughed. Then, after three or four tokes: "Doobie-doobie-do."

Across the front of the railing ran the cleaner's sign, Marvin's Cleaners, turning at the end into an arrowhead that pointed down to Marvin's door. If you leaned out you could see down to the street, but sitting back you were effectively hidden from view.

Across the horizon line a few pale pink filaments of cloud still dangled, the traffic sounds, walking sounds all gathering into a single sound that skimmed along the surface of the pavement.

"What you always hear, of course, is that we're only using twenty-five percent of our brain, though the truth is that there are three or four other brains and we're only working out of one of them. The aim of these people being to gain free access from one brain to another by way of a heavily concentrated diet, marmite, and condensed milk, and this kind of legume paste—"

For as long as he'd known him, originally at Pitt Law in 72 and 73, Gus had had the most inclusive and wide ranging, the most unreferential of raps, the strongest, most abundant, the most expensive supplies of dope. In his apogee, in the winter and spring of 73, he was importing a hundred pounds biweekly of prime Jamaican inside the cushions of footstools, until in April of that year, in Philadelphia, a city which unbeknownst to him had recently become the recipient of a large federal grant-in-aid for testing a new drug regulation program, in a spectacular 19-narc bust outside the Bellevue-Stratford which was the talk of their whole set for the next five months, he was apprehended, charged, tried, and convicted, placed on probation, and left with a $160,000 lien of taxes, against which interests of 12 percent per annum were even at this minute accruing. He worked now as a paralegal on the north side, advising tenants of their indigent rights. But he

39

hadn't changed, really. The hair was a bit skimpier, he was stouter, a little scruffier, and in general mossier, but in the manner of public monuments and statues, where wear only underlines a sense of basic permanence. The role he served in Leonard's life was likewise a monumental one, an emblem of opportunities taken, of time well spent, now sadly passed.

"But they'll be back," he assured Leonard. "People have the illusion of time going forward at a steady pace, but it moves ahead in sudden leaps, or sometimes sidewards, these past three or four years now it's been mostly backwards. You have maybe noticed this move on lately to monaural from stereo, to black and white movies and back to live TV. We'll be seeing a lot more of this sort of thing—"

The phone rang, and without a skip, barely with a pause, he picked it up and continued into it the same conversation he'd been having with Leonard—loofs and lerts, saucer landing pads in the municipal parks in Erie, the South American *dubawl* or *doombala* root, that lets you astral project, be in two places at once—

"—that all the spies are using."

Leonard began to feel a queasiness, a rising in his stomach.

"Got any Bromo?"

"Say what?"

Leonard motioned out stomach upset, need something to take.

"Try bathroom. Medicine closet."

The first glass didn't quite take, and he mixed another one, standing in the front room drinking it down and watching Gus on the porch, still on the same call, or maybe a different one now, hunched up trying to relight the roach. His place was a study in disquietudes, things misplaced and precariously balanced, a type drawer hanging over the record turntable by a single bending nail, a dartboard hung on the wall next to a frilly lampshade and a tabletop full of a lot of tiny glass objects. Painted on the window screens were busts

of solemn men in business suits and hats—so that wherever
you were sitting in the room, you were given an impression
there was somebody peering in on you.

Suddenly Gus reared back in his chair, his head flying
back, lips pointed straight up, sucking, sucking—as if his
single supply of sustenance, his sole source of oxygen, were
through this one tiny aperture.

"Gotta split."

Gus held up two fingers, either for wait a minute or else
okay—Leonard took it for okay, and went on out the door.

It was dark now, cooler than before, 8:10 and 8C by the
marquee of the Dollar Bank across the street. As soon as he
hit the sidewalk the boiling started up—he grabbed hold of a
telephone pole and turned his head away, not wanting to be
seen like this. After a minute, after two or three disappoint-
ingly small rifts, the feeling subsided, but he decided he'd
better call Geraldine, who ought to be home by this time.

First he had to wait for a booth to empty, and then the
line was busy. Geraldine worked for the consumer board, and
had advanced to the point now where all the legitimate but
irreconcilable complaints were being directed to her, with the
result, Leonard suspected, of some erosion of her sense of
professional detachment. Lately in the evenings there'd been
a series of calls from people wanting to speak to Dena, calls
she quickly terminated if he was around, but anytime he was
away from home now and tried to call back, the line would
invariably be busy. He hadn't discussed these with her yet.
They were still short of becoming an issue between them.

He started walking thumb out along the outside of the
line of parked cars, and the fifth car to come along—a good
sign, he thought, sign of a reversal in trend—an orange Volks-
wagen pulled over for him.

"I've been driving around looking for somebody to pick
up," were the first words the man behind the wheel said to
him.

He was around thirty-five and balding, but with his hair

41

splashed around in such a way as to give an impression of a
full head of hair.

"Pick up," Leonard said.

"I'm driving up from downtown and I pick up this
hitchhiker, young fellow like yourself, maybe a couple of
years younger, and my sunglasses are on the grip there. Sun
goes down, I just hang them there. And he's asking me all
these questions, about where I'm from and where I hang out,
making sure he's not going to run into me another time. And
then when I stop to let him out he grabs 'em and runs for it."

"Runs for it," Leonard said.

An oily taste was beginning to spread around the lining
of his mouth, his eyes to water, head starting to throb.

"And you know what you think, how you tell yourself,
like That's it, That's the last time for that, but I figure you've
got to resist that, you can't let yourself be poisoned."

"Poisoned," Leonard said.

"So I've been driving around—"

"Wait, stop here!" They'd almost gone by Beeler, past
his street. "I get off here."

As soon as his feet touched concrete, as soon as he felt
his knees begin to quaver under him, he knew it was that.
Poisoned. Fred's Franks. Geraldine had been warning him
about that place.

He lived almost to the top of Beeler, in one of the row
houses where Beeler joined into Wilkins. It was seventy, maybe a hundred yards to walk, most of it an upslope climb, and
with every step he could feel the prickling spread up his arms
and down the back of his legs, as the venom inched through
his system, beyond recall. He slowed his pace and slowed his
pace, fearful of the least joggling—the meat. The relish.
Poisoned.

All along the sidewalk lay piles of damp newspaper and
rusty coathangers, busted mattresses, dried-out Christmas
trees, placed out for the city pickup. As he arrived at his own
address, Leonard was mortified to find, laid out with the rest,

his isometric kit, which he still used, and the Student Prince coat he'd bought at the MGM sale in 72, and the sixteen bowling pins he'd bought for a quarter apiece last year at Goodwill and was going to sand down and varnish for the juts of the front stairs. It was the final indignity, and with it the last of his stamina faded. He stumbled up the steps to the front door and pushed the bell, pushed, and pushed again.

The first thing he noticed, watching her through the glass panel at the side of the door as she rushed to answer, was that she'd cut her hair. She hadn't told him she was planning on having her hair cut. That, and the look of pinched alarm on her face, brought him up short.

"Leonard, what is it? What's the matter?"

He tried to shosh past her—"It's all right, nothing"— but she grabbed hold of his arm and began patting him all over, shoulders, back, up and down his sides.

"Leonard, are you hurt? Leonard, what's the matter? Leonard, you're soaked completely through."

Her hair had been blonde, luxuriant, almost down to her waist, a dozen shades of amber and gold mingled through it. It had been what had given her that wild and rangy appeal, the one element he realized now, the one essential element, without which she appeared—somehow ordinary.

"Leonard, darling."

He let himself be led out to the kitchen, put on a stool, tie off, cuffs and collar open, face bathed with cooling cloths.

"Fred's Franks, Leonard, I must have warned you fifty times about that place."

He hadn't time to do more than turn his face into the sink. He hung there a minute, and then turned on the water, feeling around the rim of the basin until he found the hand spray.

"I'll bet we get a dozen calls a week about that place."

"All right," Leonard said.

"Well, there's no use knowing about these things if you're then not going to—"

"All right," Leonard said.

She picked up the phone and started dialing.

"Who're you calling now?"

"Inez."

"Don't call your mother."

"Inez knows about these things. This is what she did with the factory women in the war."

Leonard put his head back into the sink and gripped hard, imagining he was falling from an infinite height, or spinning like a pinwheel faster and faster around, or stretched out infinitely fine across a great expanse of space—trying to get a proper image for it, so that he could give it full rein and let it play itself out. There was a lengthy silence on Geraldine's end of the phone call, and when he looked over she was stretching her mouth, then her eyebrows, as if trying out new faces.

"Do—you—know—what—she's—doing?"

"I told you not to call her."

"Here I am, Leonard, my husband's dying, poisoned possibly, and every second precious, and what does she do?"

Leonard didn't say anything.

"She's been waiting years probably for this chance, for when I would have to turn to her, ever since that time I went two years to California and proved to her I could live my life without constant supervision."

Geraldine's conversations with her mother all went something like this, Geraldine on her end addressing herself to Leonard, and Inez on hers to Victor, Geraldine's stepfather. He wondered sometimes if he and Victor weren't around, if they could even talk to each other at all. He went out to the powder room under the front stairs and threw up again, sat down and took a fast, explosive shit that left his whole insides ringing, flushed, washed his face and cleaned his teeth, and sat down again for another, slower, more decorous exudation, which by the feel of it took its substance mainly out of brain matter.

He felt better now: emptied. He didn't think he was going to die now, but he was going to be sick for a while, and he started reordering the evening in his mind to accommodate the change.

The telephone rang—walls, fixtures, the hairs on the nape of his neck vibrated with the sound.

"Who's that on the phone?" he shouted out at Geraldine.

"Agnes," she shouted back.

"Tell her to call back."

No answer came to that.

A minute later, though, she appeared at the doorway with a big glass of foaming green liquid.

"Here, drink this."

"Who was that on the telephone?"

"That was Agnes. You see what I'm trying to tell you, Leonard, she won't talk to me herself, but then she calls Agnes and has her call me. Go on, drink that."

"What's in it?"

"Drink it and I'll tell you."

Leonard took an exploratory sip, then one long swallow. Simultaneously, the phone started to ring. Simultaneously, he started to retch again.

"Who's that on the telephone?" he shouted between breaths.

"Flo." He could hear her banging around the kitchen. "Leonard—I don't want you sitting down. If you're sitting or lying down, the blood is going to rush to your stomach. I want you standing so the heart will have to beat out to your extremities."

In a few seconds she reappeared at the doorway with another glass, with an inch or so of oily yellowish liquid lying in the bottom.

"Here, Flo says this'll fix you up."

"It'll have to fix the first one up first before it can get to me."

"Drink down." She was the stern, reproachful Geraldine now, saddled with a cranky Leonard. "Allll down." The telephone started ringing again.

"Ger-aldine!"

But she was off to answer it.

Leonard went out and lay down on the couch. The room was almost dark, the only light the light from the powder room, and what came in from the kitchen. The room was long and narrow, full of hulking shapes and odd angles of shadow. They'd been buying up for the next house they were expecting to own, and had too large and too much furniture.

"Who's that on the phone?"

"Mrs. Stephanic from down the block, Leonard, you're really going to have to have a talk with Victor, she's calling everybody we know."

"You had to live in Pittsburgh."

"I never said I had to live in Pittsburgh, all I ever said was"—but he managed to miss the better part of the rest of that.

Situated around the room, on end tables and on top of the television set, spread out across the carpet, were parts of a harpsichord kit which had been his and Geraldine's Christmas present to each other, that they worked on on their Friday evenings at home. The pieces were all laid out and had only to be assembled, and lying here now, he thought how much this was a metaphor of their lives together, the pieces all present and in order, but nothing adhering. Poisoned.

Single unions were binding, they told themselves, remove the bindings and the union, for being voluntary, would be that much stronger, they told themselves, what we take to another we only bring back double to each other, they told themselves.

But lately, out of negligence perhaps, out of some obscure idea of discretion maybe, out of habit as much as anything else, they'd stopped sharing with each other what-

46

ever excursions they made, so that there were now what were not misunderstandings so much as maybe just acted as misunderstandings, this accumulating sense of things unacknowledged backing up in the system. Poisoned.

"No more stuff," he shouted out to the kitchen.

Geraldine came to the doorway, silhouetted for a moment between the shadow and the light.

"No more stuff. If I wasn't dead already, I'd be dead by now from all the stuff you're pumping into me."

She jiggled her hands to show she was holding nothing.

"Moogle boogled?" she said. Moogle was her pet name for him, boogle, verb intransigent, could have variable meanings. It could mean a question, it could be a proposal. Right now it was a question.

"Moogle boogled," Leonard answered wearily.

She drifted around the room, opening the windows behind the drapes, flipping through the record albums, selecting one, putting it on the machine.

"You know where we went wrong, Geraldine?"

"No, where was that, Leonard?"

"Every step is a decision taken. No step you take can ever be taken back again. Even trying to take back a step is only another kind of moving forward."

But that wasn't what he'd meant to say—not in terms of going wrong, of what had changed. He opened his eyes to find Geraldine crouched behind the end of the couch, peeking over the arm at him.

"Moogle boogled?" she said. It was the proposal now.

Slowly, with feline stealth, she mounted the arm, easing herself down onto the cushions. She was the stalking jungle cat, he the grazing buck. Now she was the pensive doe, he the forest pond. She lipped along the flare of his nostril, the ridge of his ear, the indentation of his chin.

He didn't make a move. She unbuttoned his shirt, ran the heel of her hand two circles around one nipple, the heel of her other hand two circles around the other, the pressure of her hands pulling out lifting his shirt out of his pants. Lying here now, he began to see the evening in a new perspective. Lately, for no particular reason, they'd been slipping into periods of abstinence, a week, ten days at a time, one time for almost a full month, not because they'd argued or even that there was a reason, but lately the terminations of these sequences were becoming increasingly tentative and obtuse, the lengths he had to go to, and he imagined she too to catch his attention, more blaring and bizarre.

She undid his belt, opened his pants. Still he made no move. It was incumbent on him now not to make a move, to allow her to do everything. His penis came out flaccid. She wagged it a couple of times, smiling, a rather ambiguous smile he thought, and then slowly bent her head, her eyes fixed on his until the last possible moment. He ran the flat of his palms lightly up and down and up and down her arms, and around the back of her neck, encountering, with a jolt that turned immediately sexual, the absence of her hair, and in a second or two, without ever quite going hard, he came, a slow, even glide into green, billowing oblivions.

Sometime later he awoke chilled, his pants down around his ankles, his left leg numb from her head sleeping on his thigh, some sheets of a computer printout on the milk-to-cottage-cheese ratio in the local dairies spread across his chest. Pale gray edged the blinds at the front windows. He disentangled himself and went to the door. Outside it was just coming light, the pavement seeping puffy columns of mist, the piles of junk along the sidewalk wraithlike inside the mist, as if, like things of memory should, they were busy fading away.

He tiptoed down the steps on bare feet, but they were gone now, the jacket and bowling pins and the isometric kit, people scavaged these piles at all hours.

For a minute he stood desolate, and then turned to go back inside—and then wheeled around and raced down the length of the line scattering old sofa cushions and smashed lampshades and furnace filters out into the street, and before the first investigatory light could come on, before the next early-morning delivery van appeared at the top of the street, was up the steps and back inside—"Heh heh heh heh heh heh heh heh heh"—before she could half turn over in her sleep, back inside the arms of the unsuspecting Geraldine, Moogle Untrammable, Moogle Unchained, mad Moogle, boogling the dawn.

SYNAPHONGENUPHON

Dr. Gossner stood alone at the rear of the room, several feet back from the final row of chairs, ear cocked, as if the more attentively to follow the table of five men seated at the front.

Dr. Gossner was John Hale Clark Professor of Psychology and Head of the Department of Psychology at Pennsylvania State University, a small, sparse, silver-headed man.

The time was 3:10 the afternoon of April 5, 1972, a Wednesday, the place the Viola Room of the Cincinnati Hilton, the occasion the fifth annual meeting of the Applied Systems Association, now in its third of four days.

The topic under discussion, mechanical self-determination.

Dr. Gossner passed his hand slowly back and forth in front of his face, as if to clear from his eyes some webby obstruction. The conference had not been going well for Dr. Gossner. Just that morning he had watched a man from UC Riverside demonstrate a mechanism shaped like a fire hydrant, that could run mazes and climb a circular staircase, that duplicated, and made redundant, Dr. Gossner's own work of the past four years.

Now all his body ached and burned as though from a fever, and up the undersides of his arms was spreading a prickling burning, and in his ears a peculiar buzzing, an emptying out of sound, that he was shortly going to have to put behind him, or else turn over to entirely.

"—in this country," he heard one of the panelists say at that moment, "until we have something that can go in a car by itself and drive to Arizona."

Dr. Gossner turned a full circle around, gaping with mazed and incontinent eyes—amazed that nobody but himself in that room seemed to find anything so remarkable in those words. For him it was the moment of revelation, the moment of consolidation, "the one true moment," he would write some years later, "of inspiration in my life."

Within the hour he had reclaimed his car and started on

the drive back to Penn State; there he reassembled his staff, and within the week had begun negotiations for a new series of grants.

He taped a long sheet of butcher paper, what was to be the first of many long sheets of butcher paper, up across the front of the room, and began.

"I'm going from here to here. I'm going to tell you where we end up, and then I'm going back and tell you how we get there, and as I go along, I want to see hands of people that want to work in particular parts."

Dr. Gossner was sixty-three at the time, a man better admired for his skills of diplomacy than for any impetus to leadership. His wife had died the year before, and his daughters were both living on the west coast, and there had been talk, not too much before this, of him shortly retiring and going out there to join them. Many in the room then were surprised by the extent of what he was now proposing.

"If you're concerned about that," he said, as the first questions began to be raised, "you'd best leave now. We won't have time for rhetorical exercise here."

He had been superseded before on earlier projects, and did not mean to be superseded here. He had decided to work in sequences of ten, ten models in a sequence, each sequence devoted to a single category of performance, each model in the sequence to an individual skill. The first sequence, for instance, was devoted to standing, walking, climbing, running, to skills of mobility, the second to skills of agility, such as jumping rope and operating simple machinery, the third to articulation and ratiocination, and so on through the last, the sixth sequence, where the emphasis all was on verisimilitude, pupil fluctuation, the working of the mucus membrane.

"Gilligan."

In fact it was not until the seventh sequence that the end, or what Dr. Gossner was willing to accept as an end of the project was reached. Each sequence had been designated by a letter, and each model in that sequence by a name beginning with that letter. As the seventh model in the seventh sequence, my own designation was Gilligan-G.

"Raise your left arm, Gilligan, very good. Now your right. Look to the left, please. Now your right."

We were in Dr. Gossner's office, he behind the desk, I on a straightback chair next to the door. Sometime after this Dr. Harley, Dr. Gossner's chief associate, told me that after the fifth sequence they'd stopped dismantling the shell every time, and were just "turning a few screws and remaindering a few tapes." The remaindering was never quite complete, however, so that on this occasion I retained impressions of earlier, similar occasions. Things seemed to weave and bob about, Dr. Gossner's voice to echo in my ears.

"Tell me now, Gilligan, if you can, what name we give to a resident of Afghanistan?"

"An Afghanistanian? An Afghanese? I'm not sure," I said.

He offered no response, but went on, through another thirty-four of these questions, most of them for some reason questions of geography. A number of these I had two or three answers I could give. Eight of them I had no answer for at all. I was convinced I would be sent back for another remaindering.

But at length he seemed satisfied, and put the sheet aside.

"We've taught you to recognize alternatives," he told me. "We've taught you the limits of your own ignorance. There's not much more, I don't suppose, we can hope to accomplish than that. Listen closely to me now, Gilligan, to what I tell you."

Parked behind the building, he told me, I would find a red Ford stationwagon, and in the glove compartment of the wagon an envelope containing eighty-five dollars in small cash, and three keys. Two of the keys would operate the car, the third unlock the door of an apartment in Phoenix, the address of which I would find written on the outside of the envelope.

I was to drive to Phoenix, by whatever route I chose, arriving at that address no later than Friday noon three days hence, and wait there until he telephoned me with further instructions.

He had retained until the end that image of his initial inspiration. Now the end had come, and yet it left him curiously joyless. I can understand, of course, how he would have adopted such a manner purposely, as a precaution against unwanted controls entering into the instructions. But still, there was disappointment there. I could read it in his eyes, feel it in the way, ever so slightly, he drew back from me in his chair. I wasn't what he wanted. Oh, I can see now where nothing would have pleased him, he was an experimentalist, a laboratory man, and any end of a project would have been a disappointment to him.

But at the time I was crushed. I walked out of there despondent, down the long hallway that led to the back door to the building, past the associates and all graduate students crowded into their doorways, convinced of failure, certain I would prove a disappointment to them all.

That feeling soon dispelled, however, once I was out on the open highway. It was a warm, breezy May day. It had rained earlier in the day, but now the sun was out, and the air full with the smell of turned earth and newly mown grass. The area around Penn State is farmlands and pasture, long stretches of woodland and deep winding passes, and each new thing I encountered, every hedge and fence post that I passed, seemed to address me, filled me with exhilaration and a wild delight.

I headed south, intending to take the Turnpike west to New Stanton, and from there pick up 70 South.

As I turned up the access ramp, I passed a line of young people holding up signs that read *NYC* and *Chi WEST* and

54

Cape May NJ. Back at the laboratory, during my preinception drills, Dr. Harley and Dr. Cranston used to hold up similar signs for me, and ask me to frame the appropriate response.

I pulled up beside three girls holding a sign that said *Denver* and asked, "Would you three girls like a ride to Denver?"

That was the last I would see of Dr. Gossner, Drs. Harley and Cranston, and the laboratory for the next two years.

The girls' names I remember were Bonnie, Barbara, and Rosalie, and they were all from Rochester, New York. I don't remember much more about them than that. After I returned to the laboratory, it was thought better to eradicate my emotional capacities, with the result that all memories of any emotional bias were eradicated, too. What remain now are only some scattered bits and pieces.

I remember billboards, stretches of highway, doors and hallways; the peripheries of things. I remember riding in an open car in the hills above Mill Valley with Erwin and Colleen. I don't remember who Erwin and Colleen were exactly, or why or how long I'd been with them. I remember the date, August 22, a Tuesday.

The fog was settling in across the bay, and at one point we stopped and got out of the car and stood on the hillside watching it close in around the shoreline buildings, flying in long advance streamers up the hillside until within just a few minutes it had enveloped the spot where we were standing. We stood for some time longer, maybe for half an hour, and something was decided there, debated and decided, although I don't remember what it was.

I remember every roadside sign, every name on every mailbox on the ride back that afternoon, but not Erwin and Colleen's faces, nor the sound or even the timbre of their voices.

I remember sitting at a table in a house in Ann Arbor with six people, their faces blurred as in a photograph a thumb has rubbed the features away, when the doorbell rang, and nobody would go to answer it. Nobody would look at me, or say a word.

This was shortly after an errands android had bludgeoned a grocer to death in Santa Ana, and another run a forklift amuck in a parking plaza in Garden Park, at a time when the newspapers were full of stories about androids, and I remember as I walked to the door thinking, Here goes, here goes.

I opened the door and found Dr. Gossner standing outside, looking diminished and gray. His hair had gone completely gray, his neck and jowls, even the backs of his hands a pale, ashy gray.

"Hello, Gilligan," he said, "step outside here for a minute, won't you, I'd like a word with you."

"My name's not Gilligan," I said. "I don't know you. Go away."

"Now, Gilligan, let's not make it any more difficult on ourselves, shall we, than need be. Step outside now and we'll talk."

We walked around to the back of the house, to a point on the lawn overlooking the University of Michigan arboretum, about half a mile away. Dr. Gossner leaned heavily on my arm, every now and then pausing to regain his breath, an operation he disguised by planting it mid-sentence, as if deliberating over a word.

"I'm not going back," I told him.

"I understand," he said.

"I have my own life, my own friends, I have my own interests now."

"I understand, I quite understand."

"I choose not to go back. You gave me the capacity for making my own decisions, well, I intend to use it. I have the right to go my own way."

"I understand, I understand."

Everything I said, he nodded and agreed, disputed

nothing, raised no objections.

"In fact," he told me at one point, "your refusal to return at this point would stand in my mind as proof positive of the success of this project."

Of course I had to remember that there were others involved here too, professional people whose reputations would be hurt some of them, oh, not irreparably, perhaps—

"But don't let that deter you," he told me. "Don't let anything deter you from making the decision you're absolutely sure is right for you."

Many times since that afternoon I've wondered if there really was a decision here to be made, or if it wasn't just an instinctive part of my nature to want to do whatever it was he asked of me. As we were walking to the car that afternoon, the sun was just sinking behind the rim of the arboretum, bathing those defoliated hillsides in a soft and ambrous glow. It was the first of March, and still a little ahead of the season, and on the flat part along the base of the slopes some children had taken off their winter coats and were spinning around with them, and for a moment before I got into the car I paused, like a man going blind, recording each separate impression and separate response; for I think I recognized even then that this capacity for response, which had remained with me active undiminished since the earliest days of my inception, was something that was shortly to be taken from me, and that I was renouncing the world in a double sense of the term.

"It's for the best," Dr. Gossner said to me as we were pulling down the drive. "Things are changing out here, Gilligan. This is no place for you out here anymore, Gilligan."

a>4+<+LM=0 four

34fore

a>For weeks that followed my return, that was the
a>conversation with me, how I was better off here,

better off here than out there.

"Things are changing out there, Gilligan," Dr. Cranston told me. "A new technology comes along, people feel threatened, they feel they have to strike out."

"You were just damn lucky," Dr. Harley told me, "we came along and got you when we did."

I gathered from remarks I overheard from the graduate students that there were incidents outside involving androids, in places like Fresno and Grand Rapids, but I could never ascertain any of the details. People fell silent any time I drew near, and nobody would answer any of my questions. For a long time I was denied access to newspapers and magazines, radio and television.

Several times I appealed this policy to Dr. Gossner, but to no avail.

"We want to control what stimuli reach you," he told me. "Try to be patient, Gilligan. I know it's hard on you, but please, try to cooperate."

I resented a little the implication that I hadn't already been patient, and hadn't already fully cooperated, but I made no further complaint. When I decided to return to the laboratory, I had decided to do whatever they asked of me, to stay as long as they wanted me, to give them no cause for reproach. I let the matter of the newspapers and magazines drop.

Increasingly in the months that followed my return, Dr. Gossner retreated from the daily round of the laboratory, into the sanctity of his office, leaving Dr. Harley in charge. Dr. Harley was a taut, bloodless man, not an unkind man necessarily, but one I felt too heavily immured in the precepts of objectified logic.

It was Dr. Harley's conviction that an android should be outfitted for the need society has of it, for that much, and no more; that it be given certain mechanical skills, a pleasing disposition—and no more.

Dr. Cranston concurred with this view in substance, but

disputed it on principle. She agreed that my principal skills should be mechanical, but argued I should have imagination and a spirit of enterprise as well. Between these two there waged an unending debate.

Shortly after my return it was decided I would learn pottery making. For hours at a time I stood at my wheel, turning out planters, casseroles, full dinner services, while that debate unwound around me, sending out tendrils and branches, piercing the foundation of all consensus, until one by one it had ensnared everyone in the laboratory.

For me these were more than mere rhetorical exercises. Every few weeks one or another of the factions would prevail, and I would be carted off to the workroom, to come back out able to speak German or play the piano, or longing for nothing more out of life than to turn a wrench endlessly with a single precision motion.

Even worse than these, though, these constant re-groovings, were the occasions where discussion failed, where all experimentation ceased, and I would be sequestered to my room for some indeterminate time.

What was called my room was a space eight by fourteen feet cleared out of a storage bin at the end of the east hall. Here I had a cot, a table and lamp, a small upright locker. I had a few personal belongings, clothes mainly, and occasionally a book or two. But other than that, I had nothing.

Here, as for sometimes weeks at a time I hovered between madness and a mad sort of lucidity, I began, slowly and by arduous increment, to arrive at some measure of self-awareness.

My first recognition was of time, the proportionality of time. Time for the android, I came to see, is of two sorts, free time and allotted time. The purpose of the android is to serve man, and yet if man doesn't require service, doesn't ask, or even desire service, the android's time is his own, to do with as he sees fit. Allotted time is service time, but free time is the android's own.

This was an important breakthrough for me. Up until then, I think I'd seen myself purely as a function of my programming, an extension of whatever modality of thought had most recently been applied me, BAL over BIS, BIS over COBOL, the narrow concourses of the machine. But now I began to conceive of an existence independent of my programming, of a motive that derived not only out of form and function, that is, of my human part, but of essence and affinity, of my material self as well—of that part of me that could be factored by time. I watched the slow dance of the filament inside the light bulb, listened to the slow seasonal contractions of the walls around me, heard the deep stirrings of the earth beneath me, and did not despair, and was not afraid, for I knew that this too would pass, this time of awful testing and deprivation too would eventually pass away.

A few minutes after four one Friday afternoon in March of my second year back, I felt a sudden urge to go upstairs to Dr. Gossner's office. This was not so unusual in itself, as such timed imperatives were a daily part of my input at that time.

I opened the door and found Dr. Gossner slumped forward on his desk, in a widening pool of blood. He'd shot himself through the right temple, apparently only a few minutes earlier. Lately Dr. Gossner had been experiencing a disaster of success, his personal prominence growing as his work slipped farther and farther back from his intention or control. Rather than myself or some of the similar refined models, it was the earlier developmental models, many of them confined to single skills, which had gone into currency. Where he had thought to create a prototype, he found he had instead established a catalogue.

I adjusted his posture and cleaned up the blood, fitted a clean blotter on the desk set. I opened the bottom left-hand drawer of the desk and found a packet of envelopes addressed to different of the associates. I took these around. The name and telephone number of a funeral director came to mind. I went to a phone and called him.

The associates were grieved, but not necessarily surprised by what Dr. Gossner had done. A couple of them remarked that under the circumstances it was probably the best thing he could have done.

Only Dr. Cranston made any definite show of reaction. Reading through the letter Dr. Gossner had left her, she brought her hands to her face and began to cry. I'd always thought her a strong woman, and wondered now if I'd have to revise that opinion, or if what I was seeing wasn't only a discrepancy, an accountable feature of personality.

The afternoon following the funeral, Dr. Harley called me into his office.

"Dr. Gossner left instructions," he told me straight out, "that you be permitted to leave now if you wanted to."

"Leave the laboratory?" I said.

"For good, if you like. The choice is up to you."

In fact, he went on to say, it might be difficult keeping me here now, the way things now stood. The laboratory had been Dr. Gossner's own laboratory, staffed principally by his own people, funded largely by grants awarded to him personally.

"Dr. Cranston I understand is taking a position in Oregon. I myself am weighing several different alternatives. A number of the associates will be leaving us now, Gilligan, now that Dr. Gossner is gone."

"If I leave," I said, "will my time be my own?"

"Oh, absolutely, Gilligan, absolutely. Though there are you understand certain restrictions—"

There were restrictions on where an android could live, and where and for how many hours a week he might work, but other than that, it seemed I could pretty much go and do as I pleased.

"Though there are other options, too," Dr. Harley told me.

"What other options?" I asked.

"Well, first, Gilligan, I want you to be clear I haven't

always favored all the tinkering that's been done on you here. If I'd had my say—"

He went on for several minutes to reiterate his stand concerning androids, most of it expansions of figures I'd heard him previously employ. Like many blunt and unsentimental men, Dr. Harley was at a disadvantage anywhere a simple show of feeling would have marked the directer course.

"Suppose you go down to my basement to do your wash," he told me, "and my washing machine tears up your clothes. Am I liable? I didn't program the machine to chew up your wash." Te4y9=**synaphon**

"What none of us seems to have anticipated," he told me, "what nobody seems to have been prepared for, was a mechanism that itself would be entering into the debate." 2w/"W E =**genuphon**

"What you have to understand," he kept saying, "what I have to caution you to bear in mind, what I think is a point where our tracks are likely going to diverge." t')=

He kept shifting in his seat, pulling up and easing back. Dr. Harley had been suffering from a backache lately, what he construed to be backache, though it was in fact a cancer whose spread had now begun to penetrate his spine. He'd been waiting until this particular bit of business was over with, until he was clear and at leisure to have it attended to. In fact for the past few days now he'd been walking around with a broken back.

"Though I want you to know," he kept saying, "I don't make such a suggestion lightly." I shook my head uncomprehendingly. He gave me an exasperated look, and pushed on. "We can't keep you here," he told me, "we can't maintain you any longer. Either we have to release you, or else remainder you."

"You mean completely?"

"You would think of it more as a form of storage. And then once conditions had begun to improve—"

"No," I said, "no, I don't want that. I'll go my own way."

Immediately Dr. Harley reached into his desk drawer and came out with a typewritten sheet.

"Dr. Cranston has drawn this up. This releases you of all further obligation to the laboratory, and us of any future responsibility for you. Sign it and you're free to go."

I signed it without hesitation.

Back at my room, while I was gathering up my things, Dr. Cranston came to see me. She was dressed in street clothes, and was visibly upset.

"You have to understand," she kept telling me, "if there was anything, anything in the world else we could have done, we'd have done it."

"I do understand," I told her.

"Dr. Harley is leaving soon for Urbana. I myself am considering several different opportunities, Gilligan, there was no other course we could have followed."

"I understand," I kept telling her, "really I do."

Still she persisted, even after it must have been obvious that there was no need, and I really did prefer things this way. She was a strange, contradictory woman, and her whole style of approach was thro insistences were seen as counterproductive her insistences dismissed as mere emotionalism. Her dealings efforts d been similarly open to interpreta For my own part, Dr. Harley's attitude, it having the virtue of at least being deliverable.

Still and all, she had been a good friend to me, the one true friend I felt I had there, the only one who I felt had always held my own best interests at heart, who consistently argued for expanding my capabilities, the only one who visited me in my times of sequestering, and she was the only one now, as I was leaving, who I genuinely regretted parting from.

"Take care of yourself out there, Gilligan." She put her arms around me and gave me a hug, she stuffed some bills into my shirt pocket—"to help you get started."

"Take care of yourself out there, Gilligan, take care of yourself."

I did all right until I reached Harrisburg. Shortly into Harrisburg I came upon an android hanging by his ankles from a utility pole. His chest had been smashed open, long strands of wire and gear, all tangled and rusted, hanging almost to the ground.

I encountered them regularly after that, hanging from signal poles and nailed to the sides of buildings, FLRRS, Flurries, the four-armed variety of android designed for canneries and assembly lines.

I was wearing hiking gear, a costume that had served me well enough until now, but clearly was inappropriate for city wear. I decided to stop at a grocery, reasoning that a man carrying groceries would be least likely to be conspicuous at this hour.

It was quarter past midnight. There were eight customers in the store, and two clerks behind the counter. I moved up the first aisle, past the peanut butter and jellies, around a column of soft drinks. The store was monitored by a closed-circuit system, and every time I went by one of the cameras, the set behind the counter would flutter and spin. But I didn't notice that at first. Nor did I know at that time that such interference on such a system is one sure sign of the presence of an android.

I walked all over the store, picking up items at random, a frozen pizza, a big bag of potato curls, light, bulky items.

At the checkout counter I put down one of the bills Dr. Cranston had given me, and returned the rest to my shirt pocket. There was almost two hundred dollars there, most of it in twenty-dollar bills.

"Not in here," one of the store clerks said.

I looked around and saw a tiny old woman, of at least

seventy, jabbing the point of her umbrella into the backs of my legs. A big redheaded man came up on my right side holding out a blazing cigarette lighter. I took a step back, and another man, a littler, baldheaded man, took hold of my arm and started twisting. I'd been sent out of the laboratory with no greater strength gradation than a nine-year-old. I hadn't strength enough even to break free of his grasp.

As the flame came to within ten inches of my face, I let out a high-pitched involuntary wail, one of several involuntary alarms that had been installed inside me before I went out of the laboratory.

Just then the door swung open, and a policeman walked in.

"Come on, let's break it up." He took hold of the red-headed man's elbow and pushed his arm away. "Come on, come on here, let's give it some room."

He looked to be a man of about forty or forty-five, reserved and genial looking. He was an android. This is something I've been able to verify a number of times since then, that I can always detect the presence of another android.

"Let's move it on, bring it along." He took the bald-headed man's hands off my arm and pointed him a step back. "Come on, you!"

He grabbed me by the shoulder and gave me a hard shove toward the door.

"Let's move it out!"

His movements were efficient, unhurried. Within sixty seconds of entering the door, he had me back outside and in the front seat of his squad car. He backed around and out of the lot, drove several blocks and turned, and turned again, and headed out of town.

Another android, a female, was seated in the back.

"Where did you think you were going?" she asked me, once we were underway.

"New York. Philadelphia." Back at the laboratory one time I'd heard it said that androids were tolerated, even welcomed in the Scandinavian countries. "I planned to book ship for Stockholm."

"And they'd have had you for certain. They watch the docks and airports, all the border exchange." She reached over my shoulders and unbuttoned my shirt and began undoing my chest plate. "You must avoid the cities and towns, the public places. Keep to the mountains and woods, the open countryside."

We pulled behind a deserted gasoline station and stopped. For a minute in the shadows I could see nothing, and then I could see everything, every corner and line.

"I've disconnected your involuntaries, turned your gradations back to their maximum." She began screwing back my chestplate. "Listen closely to me now, to what I tell you."

Bending close to my ear, she whispered to me the greeting codes of the androids. Whenever I met another android, she said, I should listen not to what it said, but to the initial letters and number of letters in its words. The first letter of the first three words was the prefix, and what followed a numerical code.

When the policeman android walked into the grocery just now, for example, he used a CON code in a 423'1 sequence, and what he really said was, "Don't be alarmed. Be quiet and calm. I will assist you."

I should be especially alert, she told me, for the RLT code, the prefix for readiness. When I was conveyed those letters, I would know that the time of happy deliverance was close at hand.

She touched her fingertips to my ears, and a feeling both calming and invigorating, a feeling of wonderful confidence and assurance coursed through my body.

"Now go," she said, "but be certain wherever you go, we are close at hand, ready to come to you whenever you have need."

For a time then I wandered, moving north, moving south, however the inclination took me, tending generally in a westerly direction, every now and then stopping for a day or two, or sometimes for a week or two, and then, as the inclination took me, moving on, moving mainly by night, travelling with the dry times and the cycles of the winds. My first and longest stop was in October of that year, in Orleon in southwestern Ohio, where floodwaters had recently devastated a fifty-mile stretch of farmlands and towns. Where the waters had receded, they left behind silt and mud three and four feet deep in the streets and the basements of some of the houses. Here a willing and tireless worker was not made unwelcome.

On the edge of Orleon I built a structure eight by eleven by fourteen feet, windowless, of concrete block, a structure that might have looked outlandish in some places, but here, amid so many makeshift dwellings, scarcely merited a second glance.

To the rear of this structure I built a wooden frame eight by eleven feet, and from it hung a muslin drape, which I watched, how on damp days it hung heavy and barely moved, and on dry days fluttered in the lightest breeze. From it I began slowly to decipher the intricate patterns of the winds.

The wind is my special province. Others take as their province the rivers or the trees, but each of us serves the common mean. Only we can see the end to which an action lies, how a liter of ice, say, released into the atmosphere of Kansas today, can arrive at a thunderstorm off the coast of Thailand two weeks from tomorrow.

Only we live within the logic of the planet, in accord with the rains and tides, the subtle shiftings of the continents.

In time, as the work of reclamation began to be complete, I packed up my frame and moved on, travelling north into Michigan and then into upper Michigan, and then a long hook down through Wisconsin and Iowa and back into Illinois, tending gradually westward, every now and then stopping and setting up my frame, and then after a few days, or a week or two, moving on. From time to time messages reach me, from strangers exchanging a few words in passing, from letters and numbers stencilled on boxcars and on the sides of buildings. These counsel and guide me, warn me away from and point me toward. In Davenport I found the people all out on the streets dancing and singing, the androids did all the work. In Moline the people did the work, while the androids sang and played. These are experiments I know, attempts at conciliation, probably only the most visible out of who can say how many more.

Ahead of me now lie the last stretches of plain, the mountains, the long deserts of the west. The days are warmer now and drier, the nights longer. I cross the land inside a tornado, my feet are its touchdown, its vortex my flow. The winds are converging now, and out of their confluence there is a voice and the name of the voice is Relaytah, on whose lips I am but a single syllable, Relaytah, in whose mind I am but a single thought, Relaytah, Relaytah, the many hands that move as one.

THE GINGERBREAD HOUSE

September 30—he was coming off the turn from the Liberty Bridge when he saw her, not even her blinker lights working, standing in the drizzle in a black mink. "Don't ever think a mink doesn't still make its way in America," she told him, and he believed it. She'd sized him up immediately, known, as surely as if she'd planned it, what sort of fellow would be stopping for her, and how it would affect him. Sitting in K. J.'s afterward, leaning the slightest attentive degree toward him, bite of cheesecake poised forgotten in front of her lips, or back, arm over the back of her seat, airing out with little backhand sweeps the hair at either side of her face, he saw she would be a series of postures, a series of—photo opportunities.

She lived in Roselawn next to Frick Park, in a little fitted flagstone house—a chimney, really—concrete hoods over the windows, elaborate castiron features—a gingerbread house, nestled into the edge of the trees. The park was an old industrialist's estate, with broad, well-tended trails, and long grassy meadows completely enclosed in the trees, where you could go an hour and two hours at a stretch and not see anyone. Tuesdays, and Fridays after the second week of the month, they took long walks here, and other days for an hour or so before it got dark, down the rocky trail that paralleled Forbes as far as the Forbes Avenue Bridge, a long diagonal across the face of the hillside down to the grassy trail, and along that as far as the picnic grounds, and then a brisk, steep climb up to the meadows; or a longer, slower climb up the gully on the dirt trail that led along the stream, buggy the first week or so, and then cool and quiet, cathedral quiet, with the treetops high overhead, and birds and squirrels breaking cover along the border of their advance, and on the turns where the sunlight broke through wonderful congregations of green, as if all the green of the park were evaporated down to those few spots. He stopped, she walked on a few steps, spread out her arms, and turned a full circle around. He crossed the almost-dried-out streambed and pressed his foot against the nub of exposed root sticking out the side of the bank. The light, filtered through layers and layers of branches, seemed to drink the color out of her, her lines confusing with the lines of shale bank and trunk of a tree behind her, rock, bark, leaves, her arms and hair all the same butter-auburn, that seemed to blur even the atmosphere around her, as if she were forming out of it, along with the green, as he came closer, startling juxtaposition of green of her eyes, as if all the green of the world were refracted down to those two points. He slipped an arm around her and dropped a tiny fart, a tiny musical pair of farts—which she ignored with an indulgent smile.

She shared the house with Jim, a doctor, several years older than herself. "We share the house but there's nothing between us," she told him matter-of-factly early on, without putting any special weight on the telling of it.

She had a daughter named Marjy, age ten. "Can you believe Izzy has a ten-year-old?" people would say in genuine disbelief, and mother and daughter would link arms around each other, and bend their heads together, and smile their smile.

She worked downtown at the Gatling Institute, she was a medical librarian—although the idea was that this was more of a part-time job, she had other resources and didn't really need a job; the idea was she didn't really need you.

They walked back along the hilltop trail, catching glimpses now and again along the steep parts of spires and rooftops in Wilkinsburg and Point Breeze, first reminders in nearly an hour that the park had anything of a temporal existence. This part was more heavily populated, joggers, an occasional track team, a lot of people with dogs. The good weather had inspired a lot of people to puppies. They began as the leaves

started to fall to gain a clearer perspective on the park in relation to surrounding parts of the city, dreary after the time
changed and the weather started turning damp, and he
remembered it afterwards as a melancholy time, full of dying,
fading images, though always as a warming time, too, the
melancholy encased inside the same glow of butter-auburn
that colored even the most incidental details of that time,
that was her color, a time of particular contentment and ease,
those first weeks he met Issabeth.

October 20—he was sitting at the bar in the Tulip, eating
applesauce and stuffed shrimp and listening in on three men
bent into a tight little group in the wing of the bar. He'd
come late from work, but was stopping so that when she said
Have you eaten, he could say I ate already.

"Junior's knowledgeable but he's—erratic."
"Erratic?"
"That's the word."

The younger of the three, the one doing all the talking, was
apparently boss over the other two.

"You know, I'd like to dislike Junior, but I can't. I can't
make myself. I'd like to invite him into my home. Now, Mr.
Senior, now there's a man—"

McBride let a little of this slip by him, then: "Is this gossip?
Are we gossiping here?" One of the other men allowed as,
yes, but it was good they were getting this out. "I thought
so!" slapping his hand on the bar, "I knew we were!"—like
this was exactly what he'd been waiting to hear.

"This Mr. Senior's got something over him, a debt he's
owed his father maybe, he's inherited the business from his

71

father, I figure, and's so afraid now they're not going to accept him—"

Driving over, he'd figured out it was all right turns to her place from his, and overhead an almost full moon was shining, surrounded by an aurora ring, a rainbow around the moon, and flanked out on either side by even rows of feathery clouds spread out like battalions across the sky, and he wanted to convey precisely to her how he interpreted all of this.

"It's like the idea of God as an incompetent. It's a mistake I feel to concentrate too heavily on the omnipotence of God. He's extraordinary powers, it's true, and has his moments, but mostly's just the same as the rest of us, doing the best he can to make by."

She was down on a bedspread on the living room floor, repotting plants, and he could see her out of the corner of her eye scrutinizing him—drunk? testing me? means it?

He insisted on her coming outside. She feigned indifference, at first would go no farther than the sunporch, and then, with elaborate acquiescence, walked down to the bottom of the lawn and stood between the two lilacs with him, her head on his shoulder, heaving an occasional plaintive sigh. He became angry and was about to leave, but she brought chairs out onto the grass, and for nearly half an hour they sat, the condensation forming over the chair backs, and every individual twig and remaining leaf on the lilacs highlighted by a silvery gloss, and he told her how his parents had run away to Wellsburg, West Virginia, which had been a kind of local Gretna Green at the time. His mother gave her age as nineteen, and they wouldn't marry them without parental consent, but then when they were coming out the door an old black fellow who'd been sitting on the porch leaned up and whispered, 'If I had a car, I'd drive over to Wheeling,' and his father slipped him a quarter, which had been a pretty big tip for that time.

"Mine did the same thing," Issabeth told him, "they had these tour trains that for twenty-five dollars would take you down there, and marry you, and bring you back again, all in the same afternoon, no hotel or stopover. All very chaste, wouldn't you say?"

This was the same evening the radio was playing through all the Beatles music in alphabetical order, down now to "It's Getting Better," which some listeners had been calling in feeling ought to have been in with the G's for "Getting Better," the same evening the question was what you thought about a new national anthem, and McBride had called in and suggested "Land of a Thousand Dances."

He sat on the settee in the living room, watching her pot her plants. She was talking about Marjy, about her marriage.

"He was third of thirteen children, and my older sister is nine years older and my younger sister eleven years younger, so it was almost like being an only child. We both wanted a large family, the only disagreement being what constituted large. He wanted seven, we finally compromised on five, it was like a contract we drew up for our marriage. Though as you see we never got any farther than Marjy. His family thinks we're a horrible bust."

Had it been tough keeping track of all those birthdays?

"You know, and Duane left almost all of that to me. Mostly they fell all in January. There were the three boys, and then two girls, then four more boys, and another girl, and then three more boys, ten boys and three girls."

The telephone interrupted this—"No, no, nothing much, not too much," tucking the receiver into her neck and leaning a little to that side, "no, oh, not much, not all that much," while he thought that with them nothing much would ever happen, it would all be very nice, perfectly fine, a series of placid, eventless days. "What's the story?" they would say when they called each other during the day, "What's happening in your story today?"

Picking up the phone, putting it back down again, when she got up to leave the room and came back again, she gave him a touch, lightly on the shoulder or the knee. She was wearing a white potting apron, a kind of laboratory smock, with a man's ragged dress shirt under it, her hair pinned back with bow barrettes, one of which had come undone and was hanging only by the latch, an oddly erotic touch. Down the front of her apron ran two long gray smudges like twin loaves of french bread—as if to supply an explanation for these, she wiped her hands, backs then fronts, down the front of her apron, pushed back a loose strand of hair with the back of her wrist, gave him a little smile.

"I must have had fifty of these last April," she said, her first words after coming off the telephone, separating a sprig from around the base of a schefflera, "I gave away to people," and then for several minutes that was the last either of them said to each other.

The style of the place didn't much appeal to him. It wasn't bad style, exactly, it just wasn't his kind of style. For all the storybook extravaganza of the outside, in here was all fairly standard, Forties Elegant, all solid contours and even lines. The best probably that could be said for it was that it was the thorough working out of itself in its own terms—because he didn't think it was her style, exactly, either, it was more as if she'd given herself over entirely to the requirements of the

74

place, a quality he appreciated without being really sure that he valued in her.

She wiped her hands, backs then fronts, down the front of her potting apron, turned back the cuff of one of her sleeves, gave him a little smile.

High-back upholstery, high-stuff cushions, though not the kind you perched up on, or found yourself disappearing down into, nothing was too much, not even the stereo speakers on the floor on either side of the archway to the plant room looking too much out of place, nowhere too much of any one thing.

She was giving him another kind of smile now. She'd finished her potting now. There was a particular slowness in the way she folded up the tops of her plastic bags of peat and potting soil, gathered the spread against her and carried it onto the stoop to shake into the grass. She made a trip upstairs, and after a minute came down again and went out to the kitchen, and after a couple of minutes more went back upstairs, to stay this time he guessed. Still he sat. He'd know when the right moment came to follow her.

He wasn't tall but was solid chested, solidly built, though with some tendency toward squatness, which he compensated for, and to the same extent capitalized on with a rolling, heads-on gait, the left side of his mouth hiked up into what half amounted to a smile. He sat squat, knees wide apart, elbows braced out, and could sit indefinitely like that, that self-sure little smile on his face, through floods and famine, railing and recriminations—an attitude women took customarily for steadfastness and dependability, or alternately, signs of a secret vulnerability, that they alone could contend with.

He waited ten minutes, and then went upstairs.

The lights were all out, the only light the one in the bathroom through the bedroom. Moonlight streamed through all the windows, coating the walls and ceiling of the stairway, even the underhangs it seemed of the stairs with liquidy silver. She was bent over a hamper, he didn't think had seen him. He took his shoes and socks off outside the door and set them under the foot of the bed and was straightening up, just turning around, when she came into his arms, taking hold of his shoulders and giving them a shake—it was her way of saying she could be strong, too, could match him if the need be, though she never would, the implication was. The old style wasn't working here, was what she was telling him— though they'd pretty much worked through that part of it now, he was thinking, were beginning now to arrive at their own particular style.

It was only with her he began to think in terms of style, of himself as having a style. Like these couple of minutes on the edge of the bed after undressing, lost in rumination. She went about writing herself a note for morning, setting the alarm, examining the bottoms of her feet.

"I used to read feet, you know."

Oh, and how'd she done that?

"Oh, I'd say just whatever came to my mind. This one's for childhood—I had a different toe for each stage of life. I'd read the left foot, I remember"—ending up herself having to be the one coaxed back to the mood.

"Don't, now."

Head back, braced back, pushed up on his arms, to be hung from, clung to, "Don't," she drew him down, arms, legs, soles of her feet curling around him, blocking with her hands over his hands, her body tightening or speeding up, any movement that seemed his standard movement.

"Easy, now."

She was heavily freckled, nearly solid splotches of freckles covering her forehead and the backs of her arms, thin trails of freckle disappearing under her collar and up the rolled-up calves of her pants, and he could imagine tracing these around her body to their hidden sources and congregations—but eschewed that, imagined it was an impulse she'd seen acted on often enough by other men before, and so deliberately eschewed it, to the point of making sure that all the lights were out before he would really touch her, so that until now he'd never seen her completely naked.

"Easy, now."

Turning his head at that same moment and catching sight of the moon, just clearing the left bar of the window frame, free now of its retinue of clouds and taking flight across a clean stretch of sky, pressing his lips into the palm of her hand, her hand curved around his mouth, his chin, the tip of his nose, "Easy," like a mask, like a stalk stretching down into the root of the earth, "Easy, easy," so easy, so very easy to believe.

November 26, 3:20 p.m.—she was on the fifth, the top, a kind of penthouse floor—PH the elevator panel marked it, after which somebody had pencilled in IVE, mauve plush drapes, blond parquet floors, a huge showcase opposite where you stepped out of the elevator featuring surgical implements of the Second Sophistic. He'd imagined her shelving or cataloguing, but up here seemed all executive offices and special collections of some sort.

He found her in a little L of tiny identical offices, each with a letter, hers with an E on the door.

"Ees eet Mees Izzybess Cooper?"

She was on the phone, "You know what futility's measured in," waving him in, "futiles," framed maps of medieval Spain, a tiny pointillist in oversized matting on the walls, "You'll probably have to make new law, then, if that's the case," comic nebbishes, a brass letterholder in the shape of a giant paperclip on her desk, "No, no, I don't necessarily say that's wrong, I just say you'll have to make new law, is all," giving him the smile anytime anything pleased her on the other end. As soon as she finished that call, she started dialing again, "I have just two more to—Mary Beth Cooper calling—" He wandered out to the reception area to wait for her.

It was the afternoon before Thanksgiving Day, and all the rest of the office had already gone. The only light was what came through the open doors of the offices down the hall. He stretched out across one of the couches, picking up a magazine from the table next to him, barely able to see the pages he turned, though he knew that for the next three or four days now certain images from the advertisements, stray phrases from the articles would stick in his mind with almost mantric insistence, these last few minutes before the start of the trip—the single light on the receptionist's phone panel, the particular gloom down the little corridor of offices—the most charged, most memorable somehow of all.

They were driving to Joliet to spend Thanksgiving at her sister's, and on the way back stopping off in Ann Arbor to see his brother Steve. It was another twenty minutes before she finished her calls, and then they had to drive to Mary Pat's lot to pick up her bag out of Mary Pat's trunk, and it was 4:17 as they were starting across the Fort Pitt Bridge.

"Turn on 30, I always go that way, it's more direct."

Down a smooth, empty four-lane highway cut through sedimentary rock, that gave way once they were past the airport to an older, two-lane, heavily detoured section, that wound around gray, dilapidated farms, crossing into Ohio at East Liverpool and missing a turn somewhere and having to backtrack for eight miles, then a slow crawl through Canton, Here Lived William McKinley (1843-1901) 25th President of the United States, Bromo St., Struple St., Dunco Machine C., Orchard St. ("a misnomer if there ever was one") Here Worshipped William McKinley (1843-1901) 25th Lucky Steer lifesize replica of an Easter Island head outside the Bali Hai.

"Let's cut up to the Turnpike, we'll make up anything on time we lose on mileage."

"Let's stay this way, I always go this way, it's clear after this part."

Through a chain succession of one-stoplight towns, next to on top of every house its own chimney extension antenna pole ("like trying to reach above the environment") outside every grocery store body shop its own wheelout marquee

Girls/Women
Plush slippers
$179

and

Wicker Chairs $28
Scented Bath Oil
Jesus Savior

and tires with snowmobility and 3232 miles to Harrod's Reno.

"Let's cut up 70, we can pick the Turnpike up from there."

"Let's stay this way, I always go this way."

"So you'll try a different way, so what's the difference?"

Here it came out that she was xenophobic, had xenophobia, "though not of open spaces so much as just strange places, unfamiliar situations. You should see all I have to go through to take an airplane. Anymore, though, I think I have it mostly under control, mostly anymore it's a matter of having just too strong of preferences, a too heavy reliance on habit."

It took him a minute or two to absorb this, but then he began to think of certain insistences—certain little regularities that he'd noticed already. "That's why you always go Hobart Street."

"It would only make me uncomfortable, and I'd end up making you very uncomfortable. In a way, though, you know I think I almost appreciate it. It's as if I had my own special world, my paths all laid out for me."

He started thinking of her now as the ordered, the regulated element in his life.

"How do you see me?" he wanted to know next. She tossed him a skeptical look.

"I mean the image, what fantasy you have of me."

"I don't have fantasies of you," she said.

"I don't mean fantasy, I mean in your mind. I want to isolate what quality you identify with me."

"I don't have fantasies of you," she said.

"I imagine myself meeting you for the first time, all different ways of meeting you. You're in some kind of trouble and I come to your assistance."

"That's how you did meet me."

"I think that's why it is. You're being molested, not molested, abducted, and I come along and rescue you."

"That's what I imagine, too. I'm the kidnapped heiress and you're my rescuer."

"That's not true. You're just saying that."

"That's right."

"That's right that's right, or that's right that you're just saying that?"

This developed then into an argument, a discussion, lasting the better part of the next hundred miles, where he was saying she resisted any serious exploration, for that matter any serious kind of discussion at all—a discussion that she resisted taking seriously in any way at all.

"It's the same way you're always going into the bathroom and staying a long time. There's always some point in every evening you go into the bathroom and stay a long time, why do you do that?"

"You can't ask me that."

"It's always at a point I'm trying to establish something or on the verge of finding out something, what d'you do, just sit in there till I have time to cool off?"

"That's my mystery," she said.

"You do it to make a mystery," he said.

It had been gray the whole way, and about thirty miles before Sandusky started raining, a hard, steady downpour. They spent the night in Sandusky, having covered just over two hundred miles in a little under six hours, in the same motel where she and Duane had always stayed, a narrow concrete-block room painted enamel blue to shoulder height and lemon yellow the rest of the way around, with a blue enamel wall heater with a battered grille that McBride could figure no way of turning up any higher—spending the rest of the evening under the covers listening to the rain and the trucks go by outside. The announcers on the local TV were all modish and intense, burning with righteous indignation over pending trade embargoes and the latest county cleanup. Every couple minutes he could see her hand sliding along her side underneath the covers.

"Oh, I'm not supposed to do that, pull the skin off the bottoms of my feet."

And then about two minutes later, "I'm not doing it."

"Well then, stop doing it."
"Well, I am stopping doing it."

The next morning they drove out of Sandusky forgetting to stop for gasoline, the rain cleared now, skies sunny and bright, the highway completely deserted, all the little roadside stations closed, ten, fifteen, twenty miles, finally, at the third station they stopped at, on the dubious advice of three boys in a pickup who drove off laughing, cutting down one of the little side roads—five—six—seven miles, past bare stretches of cornfield, gray, inhospitable-looking farmhouses, set high back off the road, until finally, with less than two miles she estimated left in the tank, they arrived at the New Granada Texaco, a miniature turreted castle complete with drawbridge and goldfish moat at the intersection of exactly eleven buildings, whose proprietor, a cheery Mr. M. M. Fauganbaum, informed them had been open 365 days a year for the past seventeen years.

Most of the Thanksgiving morning segment of the trip was passed in silence.

Around Valparaiso, though, she started perking up, "That's new. All this has been built up since the last time I came through here." By now he'd settled into one of his brown funks. He knew the meaning of these moods. These were the states of mind out of which he committed all his great life's errors. "Oh, Bill's the quiet one," she told them in Joliet, leaning over the back of his chair and nuzzling his cheek, to show them he was tame. They thought he was bored. They didn't think there was that much to him. She was Izzy B. here, interested in seeing all the new malls, in what was coming up on the TV schedule.

Her sister Rosemund, called Corky, was a paler, rounder, a kind of spectrum variation of herself. The family had reached that point on the consumer scale where their means had out-run their imagination, casting them into redundancy. They had three cars, the pickup, the stationwagon, and an Impala, four televisions, two of them color, one for each of the chil-dren's rooms, and five telephones, including one out in the greenhouse.

"Have you shown Bill your greenhouse yet, Norman?" Corky asked her husband at breakfast their second morning there.

The greenhouse he'd spotted already, a long chicken coop or shed caddycorner the garage, with thick sheets of opaque plastic tacked up the sides.

"Why, noo, see I can't get him to sign the paper where he won't use his camera"—he liked that, the place steamy and comfortable even in its winter's desolation, the shelves hung down from the ceiling by their special assembly of wires, the big bags of peat and potting soil he recognized as the mother lode for Issabeth's little bags, and the obvious pride showing through, in how many of this and flats of that were sold each year, and the people who pulled up out front even before the sign went out, and the burners that could raise the temperature to eighty degrees within half an hour on even the coldest of days.

And Saturday they took the tour through Joliet, the boarded-up storefronts, crumbling pavements downtown, and then the boom in the peripheries, giant shopping plazas, vast new apartment complexes going up—and that he'd liked, the American urban crisis in microcosm.

The afternoon before they left he heard her in the basement, where she was helping her sister sort the wash, telling her, "If ever there's anything Bill doesn't like, he just doesn't get involved. McBride's got his getting by down pat."

"He's lazy," Corky suggested.
"No, Bill's a good worker. Anytime he starts something, he's sure to see it through. Right now we're buying a new pair of boots. Monday we actually brought a pair home with us, but Tuesday they had to go back again. We have the style we're looking for now, but the color's still not quite right."

He was in the first-floor powder room, bending over to turn a page in one of her brother-in-law's magazines, and this came out the register, oracular, portentous.

"His mother buys all his underwear," she said next. "Oh—she gets a nice kind, nothing fancy, but a good kind."
"Not this kind with the red stripe around the waist," her sister said. They had a little laugh over that. "They say that kind's not good for them. It gets too hot in there for the sperms and it kills them."
"Oh, that's no problem Bill ever has. I never saw a guy come so much. He's already got one woman pregnant, and

she was wearing an IUD.''

It had been snowing for almost an hour when they started out Sunday morning. The plan was to stop off in Ann Arbor and have dinner at Steve's, and then drive on through to be back for work on Monday morning. But they hadn't gone more than three miles on the Interstate when they came upon a four-rig, five-rig pileup—the severity of it in their own uncertainty as to how many were involved. "Scots Towels," Issabeth said, turning around on the seat to read the cartons strewn along the guardrail. "Momento mori," McBride said, noting the particular red of the flares, the glitter of smashed glass, criss-cross of tire tracks on the snow, the peculiar aesthetics of the moment.

Every two or three miles after that "one every five miles the past hundred miles" they passed cars "surprisingly few trucks on the highway now" skidded into the trough, one of them just three or four cars ahead of them that just suddenly turned and sailed off the embankment, as if deliberately, "like he'd just wanted to stop there for a rest."

By the time they reached 94 it was bumper-to-bumper, twenty-five, thirty-five, never more than forty the whole day, two solid lines of taillights disappearing into, two more of headlights ghostly reappearing out of the white, "like driving into an impressionist painting."

At the reststops the people were all smiling and congenial, all normal reserves suspended for the duration.

"I'm headed here and here's where we're at now," one man at the map told them, "and here's where I started from, that was ten o'clock this morning, first, see, I had to drive my brother over here to pick up his van—"
"You change lanes," a man behind them said, "and it's

half an hour before you can get back in again."

"Ain't no use," another man told him. "Neither one's any faster. I counted one yellow van I passed sixteen times."

By now they were barely speaking, the ultimate test, he was thinking, simply in how many miles you can clock together, the distance factor, an element much underappreciated in precis of the contemporary relation. She spent most of her time dozing with her head wedged into the space between the seat and the door. Every half hour or so the windshield wipers iced over, forming fat icicles that wetted rather than cleared the glass, and with this much traffic there was no way you could pull over and clear them and then get back on again, and there was a leak of cold air from somewhere underneath the dash that he was no way able to pinpoint or shut off. It was the first trip in the new car, and he was still concerned with determining what were its strong and its weak points. By nine that evening they were still over fifty miles outside of Ann Arbor, and it wasn't until here he started thinking that this was how it affected her, her xeno-phobia, she'd never come this way before. It was like Uta in the kitchen with her thunderstorms, the time he'd walked out to the kitchen and she had her arms down on the counter, and when he asked what was the matter had snap-ped at him, "Oo! leave me be!"

He began to be more solicitous toward her now, reaching over to pat and rub her shoulder, until she blurted—"you—stop—that!" It was the same kind of thing.

It was eleven o'clock by the time they reached Steve's, Stephen he wanted to be called now, another gingerbread house—squarer, squatter, set on the fallaway of a long sloping lawn, with stone steps leading down on either side to a matched gazebo in the back. It blew him away, the idea of the two brothers both living in houses like that, each one involved with women who owned houses like that.

The two brothers grappled and skidded across the lawn, grabbing big handfuls of snow off the evergreens and hurling them at each other, while she drifted around the borders of the property, trailing fingertips along the trunks of trees, around the fat concrete pillars that held up the porch.

Stephen's Lisa had walked out on him two nights earlier. "What can I tell you?" helping them in with their things from the car, "It isn't as if it comes exactly as any surprise. It's not like there hadn't been things I might not have done that couldn't have prevented it—but what can I say?"

"There's nothing you can say," McBride told him.

But he was obsessed with it, fixing them something to eat, hunting out a place for them to spend the night—"which isn't to say I don't still think it's not the best thing either of us could be doing at this point, whatever I might happen to feel about it personally. I just couldn't say."

They slept on a mattress on the attic floor. Stephen was turning the attic into an office, and all but a square of boards in the middle of the floor had been torn up, and there were planks stacked all around the walls, and even after they were under the covers and the light was out, he sat on the ladder leading up there, only the top of his head visible above the trapdoor—"which still doesn't mean if she didn't show up at the door right this minute, I might not still take her in, I just can't say."

"And the funny part is," McBride told her after Stephen had gone down, "I've never even met the girl. That's what the trip was supposed to be all about, for the two of us to have a chance to meet each other."

Even after he'd gone down, they could hear him moving around downstairs, opening and closing cupboard doors, trying to play the stereo down low, the house acting as a kind of vibraphone picking up and carrying every tiny movement and sound from one end to the other—it was this, they decided, that was probably the prime cause of the breakup, this "surfluit of intimacy."

Before they could go to sleep that night, she had to hear everything there was to know about the two brothers, where they'd played as boys, their first cars, first double dates, adding that much more to the territory she could safely traverse in him. The attic was unheated, save for an antiquated space heater that they dubbed Granny Grumps, that kicked on with an exasperated roar every ten or fifteen minutes through the night. The windows were at floor level, and laced around the edges with frost, and out under the streetlight they could see it still snowing, their lips close to each other's ear, and every little rustle and turn telegraphing through the boards, the necessity of keeping still building an erotic hilarity, the stifling of which made only more explosive, the shadows of the planks shifting in the heater glow like processions of monks circling the walls, like fantastic forests blooming and decomposing all around them, and he remembered it afterward as the best time of the entire trip, as one of their finer times, a time they were closest and most giving.

In the morning, Stephen, guilty over going on so long about one thing, tried drawing her out, where she was from, where she'd gone to school, what sort of position she envisioned for her life. Here she was the quiet one, rubbing her finger along the rim of the cinnamon can, both brothers liked a lot of cinnamon on their wheatcakes, shrugging and shaking her head, like this was all no more than a matter of opinion, on topics on which she had no particular opinion.

"Gee, Bill, she's a swell looking girl," Stephen told him as they were carrying the things back out to the car, "but doesn't she ever say anything?"

"She's abnormally self-possessed," McBride told him. "She's always making people nervous. She brings into question their whole version of reality."

It was snowing up now, the wind lifting ragged swirls of white off the rooftops and tops of cars, as if they were smoldering. They were nearly two hours to Toledo, but once they were past Toledo and out on the Turnpike, it started tapering down, and by Exit 6-Fremont they were out of it entirely, they'd outrun the storm. Within just a few minutes he could begin to feel a change. "I've seen that before, I've been this way before," she said, smiling and stretching like somebody coming out of a heavy sleep.

"—I had the key, I had the key and was to go in just to reset the alarm, there was another neighbor would hear the alarm and then would telephone me—"

Still the silences continued, fifteen, thirty minutes at a stretch, little retooling stops where certain small kicks and abrasions in the relationship were or maybe were not being greased out.

It was nine-thirty that evening when they reached Pittsburgh. It hadn't snowed at all here, wasn't even down to freezing, hadn't even rained over the weekend here. He dropped her off and went back to his place to shower and change, and by the time he returned, about an hour later, some sort of subtle shift had occurred. He could feel her following his moves, marking them down against some vagrant bill of particulars he was going shortly to be presented with.

Jim was in Somerset for the week and there was half a cheesecake and an almost full bottle of wine in the refrigerator. They built a fire in the living room and spread out in front of it. He watched her as she got up and moved around, her fingers browsing the furniture backs, along the spines of the books on the bookshelf, reclaiming, reacclimating herself. How many of her gestures he'd seen previously as quirky or distinctive, he thought of now as merely territorial.

He lay propped on one elbow, she leaning back into his shoulder. She'd changed into a blue terry robe and tied her hair back in a ponytail after her shower, the only time he'd seen it worn that way, the ends spilling over onto his arm, and he lay sorting through the different strands, the russets and pure reds, and down the blonde scale almost to pure white. Every so often she turned her head as if about to speak, though for long stretches neither of them did. The silences continued, mellower now, ripened into a kind of private language. They'd discovered their natural medium on this trip.

Presently she got up, "I think I'll go up now." He looked up expectantly. She walked as far as the bottom of the stairs, and paused there a moment, and smiling said, "You know, I like to think of myself as pretty unoutfigurable, but you're making such a patient study, I'm afraid that pretty soon there'll be nothing left to unravel," and still smiling, went on up the stairs.

For a while longer he continued in front of the fire. He'd answered nothing because her words had put the situation in front of him, and he was absorbed in looking at it. He'd been watching her long enough, was what she was telling him, long enough for it to be apparent and her to know what it meant. It meant he couldn't decide—though why he couldn't decide was a major problem in what he couldn't decide, or what he couldn't decide in why he couldn't decide, he wasn't sure which.

In fact he'd been seeing this coming for some time now, this feeling of a necessary next step that he, or in her mind at any rate, had been unwilling or maybe just unready to take, a step that needn't maybe be taken so much as just acknowledged, and the conditions under which it be taken worked out and agreed on between them.

It wasn't that he was afraid of any attachment, afraid of an attachment with her turning out to be too binding an agreement, the lightness of any hold he'd yet been able to affect over her gave an ample contradiction to that, or of this turning out to be too congenial, too accommodating an arrangement, he felt that probably any kind of arrangement they worked out now would suit him about right at this point, even if it came down to losing her, which had to be a good part of the problem right there, that he could conceive of losing her, plan with it in his mind, and not be burning and ranting even at the thought of it, had to denote some essential lack of flame in their relationship.

But he thought of certain moments, certain glimpses she'd afforded him of herself, and how in fifteen minutes, or fifteen seconds if he wanted it, he could be up those stairs and in her arms, and how all of this here tonight, this whole past problematic weekend, might only in some circuitous way have been preparation for delights unexampled and rare, that waited him even now at the top of those stairs; how none of this might be anything more than a too-analytic turn of mind, making of every consideration a complication, of every speculation an imperative, to so disproportionate a degree that any solution offered was likely inevitably to appear insufficient, he thought it very well could be that.

His picture of her had been changing on this trip. It wasn't that anything had been added to it or taken away, but that certain factors, certain facts of their relationship, like the fact of her having a ten-year-old, or the fact of her being four years older than he was, facts he'd already recognized and placed in importance, had suddenly taken on a new level of importance, or certain remnants of her marriage, that he didn't think any kind of arrangement was ever quite going to eradicate.

Not that Marjy in herself was any problem, Marjy spent most of her time with her father now, the result of some sort of mysterious backplay that'd been going on around the time he first met her, and maybe accounted for this coming to him now, the first, safest harbor outside the storm. Which was a large part of the problem in itself, that this was something coming to him, being put in front of him, instead of just always being there.

But that would be her way, he could see now was always going to be her way. She would always have to have the boundaries drawn, her paths all laid out. It wasn't that his picture of her had been changing, but that the initial impressions he'd formed of her had now been verified, his early conception of her had now been filled in by particulars, so that he'd lost his concept, to a certain extent lost his understanding of her, in a real sense he had lost her already.

For a while he'd been able to hear her moving around upstairs, in a horseshoe arc over the archway into the plant room, where he imagined the bed to be, to a spot almost directly over his head, pausing there a minute, calculatingly perhaps, while he was to lie down here wondering what she might be doing up there, and then back over to the bed, and for a long time now nothing. The clock in the dining room was working its way a second time around its chimes, the fire burned almost down to embers and a winter's chill begun to creep its way across the floorboards—as he got up, he reminded himself to check the thermostat before going upstairs. It was ten before two as he started up the stairs, thinking to himself that in one sense his problem would already be solved, she'd be asleep by this time, thinking if all this he'd been thinking here tonight were true, he'd picked the worst, the course least guaranteed to appease, thinking how it was all of a piece with his life, this reluctance in the face of opportunity, this conscientious instinct for fucking in the face of whatever was going right in his life, and if it was that here now again, he was finished, because he'd lose it here, was what she was telling him, if he kept up like he had here tonight and this past weekend, he was going to lose it sure.

While he was undressing, though, bent over the bed to pull off his shoes, with her sleeping only a few inches from him, her hair unfastened and spread across the pillow, another thought came to mind—her fingers tangled up in the alarm cord, head, shoulders, and arm concisely framed between two narrow diagonals of moonlight, and all his doubts of only a few minutes earlier already blurring in his mind, he saw this would be gotten by. These doubts, these fears, these reservations were only abstract, nebulous, he would put them aside, just as she would put aside the fact of ever having noticed them, and they'd go on, happier, no doubt, and more content, the first perhaps of many such compromises and denials, forgetting in time no doubt they'd even had any doubts at all.

5:15—what woke him first was the cat, Jim's cat, rubbing and pushing against his face. The cat had never bothered with him before, and his first thought was that he'd gotten into the

wine glasses they'd left out downstairs. And there was this
insistent ringing in his ears, that no amount of answering
could keep cleared. A bird had dropped down the flue plug-
ging the vent, and with the fireplace going it hadn't been
until they were already in bed that the thermostat had kicked
on. He had another recollection, too, dimly, as if from some
other evening, of her shaking him and saying I smell something funny, and his saying It's only the mills close the window, and her saying It's closed already I'm getting out of
here, and something in her *out of here* that had alerted him.
She was smaller, and the ringing had gotten to her first, and
she had strength enough to waken him but not enough to get
out herself. Through all of this he thought of them as on a
shared venture, of her having brought it her part of the way,
and now it up to him to carry it the rest. She'd walked into
the closet to put on a robe or else mistaking the door, and
there was a minute now where she wasn't in bed and he
wasn't able to call out for her, and what went through his
mind was another memory, repressed until now, of the night
when he was eleven years old when their house had caught
fire, and he'd had to drag his mother screaming and fighting
him the whole way out to the street, it was that same experience here but in another form, in each the pitting of his
fading resources against a maximum resistance, here a maximum lack of resistance, and only the memory of the urgency
of that other occasion that impressed on him the urgency
here, so certain was his instinct just to lay down his head,
close his eyes for just a minute, until the tearing could stop,
so shifting and dreamlike were all the shapes around him, and
the feeling like in a dream of pushing and pushing and still
going nowhere. By the time he'd gotten her as far as the top
of the stairs, he realized that what he should have done was
open the bedroom windows and put the exhaust fan on in
the bathroom, it would be getting thicker now as they went
down, but the bedroom windows were the narrow crank kind
that he didn't think you could even get a head through, and

the bathroom fan had been busted a week ago, and he doubted would have been attended to by this time. Through all of this his mind remained remarkably lucid and clear, figuring out chances, measuring options, against the sinking, and the lassitude, and the awful weighing, his wrists so heavily weighted he could barely lift them off the carpet, his eyelids so laden it was all he could do, trembling and straining, to keep them open the barest slit, having to feel his way along the banister poles, down over every stair tread, convinced the whole time he'd taken a wrong turn and was only leading them down some irreversible digression, hearing in his ears the whole time her words at her sister's, "Anytime Bill starts something, he's guaranteed to see it through," as though she'd prepared him, anticipated this moment and prepared him to meet it.

He had no recollection of getting them out the door. He took her through the kitchen and out the back way, although the front door was only a few feet from the bottom of the stairs and would only have been that much nearer. It was snowing outside. It had just started, fat, sticky flakes batting his eyelashes and cheeks. It was the Michigan snowstorm caught up with them. Coming down the back steps, his legs gave out and he came down hard, giving her a push as he fell so that she landed in the grass. There were no lights on in any of the houses around yet.

There was no breath. Her nightgown was ripped away from one breast, the nipple puckered and green, and around it pale clusters of freckles faded and pink like disease spots— "Kaoork!" coming out ridiculously puny and ineffectual— "Kaoork! Ka-ka-oorrrk!" pawing with his fingers at the grass.

His only thought was to keep the snow away from her, gathering her up in his arms, gathering up handfuls of her hair, wiping her cheeks and forehead with the point of his chin, pressing her tight, forearms locked against the ridges of her back, pressing, pressing, and gradually releasing, ten minutes, fifteen minutes, long after the point where reason alone would have told him to quit, until a tiny bubble, blue and rainbow tinged, popped at the corner of her lips, followed by a thin trickle of oily foam.

"Oh my god oh my baby oh my precious!"

Scarcely with a pressure now, working and pressing, until she stirred, and began to climb up into his arms, and then, as if that much effort alone had depleted her, slipped back, her head dropped back, her whole body going lax in his arms. Nowhere did he feel closer to losing her than he did here, as he crouched, down on one knee with her full weight across his opposite knee, not daring to make a move, one of her arms akimbo around the back of her head, but not daring a move to correct it, as a minute, two minutes, a hundred minutes it seemed drifted by, while the snowflakes quietly gathered onto her eyelids and cheeks and into the trough between her breasts, barely melting there, and only the faintest and most deferential of pulses beat in the vein along her neck.

Then a long halt like a sigh, and she was pushing away, turned her face and coughed something into the grass, which she covered with weary scoops of her hand.

"I don't think if there hadn't been two of us either one of us would have made it."
"Don't try to think that now."
"I kept dreaming I was hanging on you and you were trying to pull away from me and I kept dragging on you."

He held her then, just held her for a few minutes, his hands pressed flat against either side of her face.

96

Then they staged a small re-enactment of the same rescue with Domitian the cat, McBride going around this time opening windows and doors, and down to the basement with a wet towel over his face to turn off the valve, and when he came back out she was up on hunkers, trying to sort out her nightgown.

"You know they say if you save a life you're responsible to them forever."

But it wasn't clear if she was kidding now. She got onto her feet, though wobbly, insisting on going back inside. McBride walked with her as far as the door and stood there a minute while she went around with his coat over her shoulders, fanning the air with a towel, then he walked down to the end of the drive to watch for the first light to come on.

His feet left bare circles on the concrete behind him. Above the roofline on the other side of the street there was a lightening, a greater distinguishability of shape that prefigured the dawn, or maybe was just this morning's version of daybreak. He'd pulled on trousers and a pair of shoes while he was inside, and in his T-shirt and no socks stood shivering and rubbing his arms, taking deep, steady breaths. A dog padded by, with many a reproachful sidelong glance, keeping a seemingly straight course down the middle of the street but leaving behind a widely meandering track. Out on the avenue a couple of delivery trucks flashed by—but he was waiting for a definite sign, the first wakening light to come on, somebody else up and moving around, not knowing about the snow yet. After a while he was just waiting—and then the big plate-glass at the second floor front of the big yellow brick two up on the other side came on, followed in a minute by a small oval stained-glass on the side a couple down on this side, that may have already been on. He stood a moment or two longer, noting the way the dog tracks already blended in

97

with the rest of the scene, the snow still lying on top of the grass, the two baby maples in the lawn directly opposite with the red nursery tags hanging from their lower branches; then he walked around back.

The outside air had cleared his lungs enough so that the smell was detectable again, and he couldn't bring himself to go back inside just yet. The ringing had diminished, but grown somber and more authoritative, and there were the beginnings of a souring after-effect, the rooms shabby and grainy in this light, and her with his suitcoat over her night-gown looking frumpish and drawn, batting the air with a bathtowel. Seeing him standing there, she stopped and gave him a smile—a strange, gloatish smile—and what that was sup-posed to indicate, what any of this might indicate, what lay ahead for them now—he hadn't any idea.

You take my skin,
I take your bone.
You take my bone,
I take your life.
                    —precept of Shotokan Karate

SKIN AND BONE

Tuesdays they practiced upstairs in the women's gym, and sometimes there he felt it, if he'd done particularly well that night, into April and May after it started staying light later and the windows could be open—the oneness with the stance you were supposed to feel, a loosening of muscles and easing of the pain, not a diminishing of it exactly, but going beyond it, into an almost druggy transcendence where colors, shapes, the surfaces of things became abstractions of themselves. Thursdays, and Saturday mornings during wrestling season, they practiced downstairs in the fencing/volleyball room, where there were score markers and notices all over the walls, and street sounds coming through the windows, high, frosted-glass windows flush up to the ceiling, with chicken wire embedded in the glass, and some elaborate crank mechanism for opening and closing them that ran down the side of the wall. Upstairs they were at the back of the building, looking out onto a wooded hillside, with stretch bars and full-length mirrors, and enough floor space for separating the beginners' from the advanced groups.

Tuesday, ironically, was the night Emil led practice—ironic because Emil was the one Tim considered the most rootbound of the blackbelts, a stocky, and for all his conditioning, somewhat chunky graduate student in either mathematics or physics, with a bright, unflagging smile and a sparse tuft of sandy hair curling out of the hollow of his throat. "I *want* you to improve," he would tell them as he went around correcting postures. It had been Emil the winter before who, with the flu and a temperature of 102, came in anyway, just

99

to prove he could overcome it, running four miles outside barefoot by himself before practice, and then leading the club through five hundred side thrust kicks, five hundred side snap, at least a thousand roundhouse kicks, ending the evening with fifteen minutes in *kibadach*—all low leg exercises, Tim noted. This was just about the time Tim was starting to get over the trouble he'd been having with his knees.

"This is crazy," he told Dietz.

"This is what you gotta do," Dietz told him, "if you want to be ready for special training."

The special trainings were a recent innovation, weekend-long retreats held bi-yearly on the campus of a community college outside the city, three and four intensive two-hour practices a day, with special surprise sessions thrown in at five in the morning—a little like hell week in the fraternity Tim was thinking, watching it all from a detached perspective, the mounting enthusiasm, the growing rigor of the practices as the big time drew near, the pressure on everybody to sign up, go along—"If anybody doesn't have the twenty dollars," Emil told them after two separate practices, "I'll give him the money out of my own wallet"—and then afterward, the esprit, the camaraderie, the casual ostracism of those who hadn't gone by those that had.

(Around this same time, too, there was a move to federate the different clubs around the country, accompanied by a five-dollar raise of dues, and shortly after that, by the appearance, at fifteen dollars a copy, of the English translation by the American head of the school of the founder's autobiography, after which all the stances had to be revised downward, and for the next three months the brownbelts would be every five minutes breaking off practice to run over to the coatracks to consult a copy on some point of dispute.)

It was a Tuesday, three weeks before spring special training, that Esther appeared. She walked in five minutes before time for practice to start, crossing the floor with solemn, self-contained steps, her brown belt over her shoulder. She put

100

her bag down by a pillar, tied on her belt, and stretched, walked out to the middle of the floor and breathed and stretched, sank down into a full split, turned left, and then right, and then over into a plow, which she held, unmoving, until the call came for bowing in.

A nice sense of theater, Tim thought.

She wore a *gi* of a lighter fabric, a couple of shades whiter than those of the club, the jacket loose fitting, accentuating the slimness and narrowness of her line. She was around twenty-four or -five, tall, around five-nine or five-ten, with brown hair parted down the center and clipped behind her ears with bow barrettes of red and yellow molded plastic. Sparring, she went through some stylized breathing routine, giving out a growl every time she made a punch. The first time Tim stood up to her, he broke up, which infuriated her. After each set of punches, she rehearsed back over the final one to herself, as if to imprint its deficiencies on her mind.

Mr. Shuri was there to supervise that evening, a distinction in itself, and after bowing out, he raised a hand for further courtesy.

"Tonight back from former Europe pretemper Esther Hardy."

He heard later that she was a remote descendant of British novelist Thomas Hardy, another nice touch Tim thought. She was a past member of the club returning after two years in Europe, where she'd trained with Didier, who was a former fellow or esteemed former pupil of Mr. Shuri's. Every eight or ten words Mr. Shuri lapsed into a shrugging inarticulacy, a little gathering in and back that was more expressive, more lucid finally than any words could be. What came across most was the *gentilesse* of the man, a sense of good meaning and design—though a certain part of that Tim had concluded had to be written off to simple inscrutability. For a long time he'd been thinking he'd been telling them to "Excel! Excel!", a suitable enough exhortation he'd thought, until he realized that what he really was saying was, "Exhale!

Exhale!"

Called upon herself to describe her experiences abroad, Esther was similarly inaudible, speaking out of a modesty that confined itself to whispers. Tim passed the time scanning the new beginners' group, sprawled out across the lower end of the floor, gaping at her as if a berserk had been set down into their midst—figuring out which of this assorted rape bait and bully fodder would be the ones most likely to stick it through, which ones would prove the real *aficionados*, measuring the distance between them and his own beginners' class of two years ago, many of whom, and of the three or four classes since then, had long since passed him by. She was a carpenter, had apprenticed to a cabinet maker in Belgium.

"She's trained in France," Dietz told him afterward in the showers, "she trained in Spain, she's trained all over Europe. She trained with Didier." Dietz's tone said that while he recognized that her commitment was strong, he could never take any woman's commitment fully seriously. "They wouldn't let her apprentice here so she went over and did her apprenticeship there and now she's suing the union." His tone said he thought she was a troublemaker.

"The training in Spain is mostly overcoming the pain," Tim suggested—but Dietz had his head under the shower and probably didn't hear that. Dietz wasn't large but he was powerfully built, and he worked exceptionally hard. He could bring his leg up and hold it alongside his head, and was the only one of the brownbelts Tim considered really able to do the roundhouse—although the fact that he could see him doing it probably suggested that he wasn't doing it properly, the true level of technique, the blackbelt's level of technique, being always undetectable. A fringe of dark hair, smoothed down by the water, outlined the curve of his buttocks, hard, almost grotesquely rounded buttocks, his whole body firm and sharply articulated, as if he'd been conceived on a heroic scale and then reduced down to everyday size. He snapped his head back and shook it side to side doggy style, spraying water the width of the enclosure.

Tim said, "I had this dream last night where there was this temple on the beach, a training school, and all the rocks were painted, and the principal design was this big mouth eating pussy. And all the acolytes were ambulatories, cripples."

Dietz, taking this for a confidence, returned it with one of his own, "I've been going without sleep lately, just to see how long I can do it. You know if you don't sleep, you don't need to sleep at all. It's just a habit people get into. I've made it four days so far."

In the past he'd confided similar projects to Tim, like his method for curing a fear of heights by climbing a 40-foot stepladder a step at a time while reading Descartes' *Rules for the Regulation of the Mind*, or his conviction that old age and death are the products merely of inattention, the toxins entering the body at the first age of maturity, twenty-one, twenty-two, the age he was coming into now, and the thing to do was never to let your guard down and allow them to get in in the first place. He was convinced he was going to live forever, he was a fanatic, that one element of fanaticism, Tim recognized, recognizing it as what was missing in himself, the feature that led him to excel.

He took his time dressing, taking slow pleasure in the buttoning of a button, the tying on of a shoe, waiting until now, until he was about to leave the building, to make his visit to the water fountain. Ten short sips, and no more. Not to put too much cold water on the stomach so shortly after practice. Just inside the door the three Buckley kids were waiting for their father to come get them, the younger of the girls, Little Eva, the infant prodigy and sweetheart of the club, a brownbelt at age nine—and it was said that Mr. Shuri was holding her back for fear of advancing her too early. Under the shadow of her example the other girl and the younger brother, both of them bespectacled and hopelessly awkward on the floor, were taking on more and more of a

whipped appearance, hanging listlessly against the sides of the
Coke machine, while she stood up straight and tall at the
door, bidding a smiling good-night to each person as they
went out.

"Good practice."

"Good practice."

Outside there were still a few people sitting on the
railing, and on the wall along the bottom of the steps waiting
for their rides. As he came down the steps, Tim could hear
Oster describing someone apparently from another school,
who "held his fist against his chest, and just turned it like
that, and he was flat out on his ass." There was an active
cornball element running through the club, evidenced in a lot
of breathless stories about men wrestling the horns out of live
bulls with their bare hands, and a lot of sly little jokes with
shindigs in the punchline. It was still light, still mild outside,
the evening carrying over into it something of the balminess
of the day, the first good day almost of the season. A slow
April and chill rains the first week of the month had retarded
the budding, and now it was as if the whole world was in
bloom simultaneously, the evening fragrant with surreptitious
possibility, a kind of evening where opportunity has its
thumb out on every street corner. From behind a building on
the other side of the street a voice called out and another
answered, not quite coalesced into voices yet, more still man-
ifestations of a mood, the row of maples across the street,
each with the bulb of a streetlamp in back of its shrub, a
trail of glittering starbursts leading in even diminution into
the darkness of the park. He'd left his car at the bottom of
the park next to the coal memorial, but took a more round-
about route up the golf course and over the ridge, along the
rim of a wooded hillside that paralleled Cornwallis Avenue.
Just over the crest of the ridge was an old estate that for the
past several years had served as an arts and handicraft center,
and in the summers as headquarters for the park mimes. The
main building had recently been torn down, but the founda-

tion walls and a section of formal gardens were still intact, bordered on the right by a line of five semiruined archways, in the intervals of which were mock arches in which there were stone benches. In the shadow of the second of these there was a figure, a pair of figures were standing—automatically he shifted his bag around to his back and angled out to the left, mediating a course between the arches and a clump of lilacs on his other side, gauging as he moved how many steps it would take to land a lunge punch into that evergreen, a side snap to the trunk of that tree, elbows close, arms loose at his sides, taking quick, purposeful steps. Just beyond the arches was the opening of a drive that led down the hillside to the street. It was here he was making for.

Halfway down the hill, where the drive made a sharp turn just before dropping to the street, a figure in a blue jersey, that he hadn't spotted until he was right on top of him, turned out of the bushes zipping up his fly.

"Hey, good lookin," Tim said as he was going by, "whatcha got cookin?"

That slowed him down. He was a young guy, about twenty-two or -three, not too tall but nice built, slim built, with dark hair and a bushy moustache.

"Hey, what's happening, hey, you got a match? You live around here? Say, you wouldn't happen to have the time, would you?"

The young guy laughed and said, "Na, hey, I'm down here waiting for my bus, I just came up to take a leak is all."

Tim took a step in then back.

"Hey, you need a ride, hey, come on over here a minute, I'll give you the world tour."

"Na, hey," the young guy said, "that's all right, I'm too busy right now." He took a couple steps down the hill, but didn't quite break away.

"Hey, hey, nice arms, umm, like those big arms. Hey, hey, walk over here a minute, take a walk over here, I've got something I want to ask you."

"Na, hey," the young guy laughed and rubbed his stomach under his jersey, but in the end said, "that's okay, I gotta meet my bus," and went on down the hill.

For a while Tim hung around the edge of the street light—once he looked around and saw him standing there, and then didn't look around again. He let two buses go by. Perhaps neither one of them was his. Tim walked back to the top of the hill, where the same two figures were still standing in the shadow of the arches, and another one now along the side of the foundation wall, which he reconnoitered, and as he returned to the head of the drive he caught sight of a figure in a blue jersey cutting up into the trees just this side of the turn. Tim was right behind him.

Afterwards they sat on the trunk of a fallen tree sharing a smoke.

"How come you're like that?" the young guy wanted to know now.

"It's my nature," Tim told him. "It's how I am."

"I mean were you always that way? Didn't you ever try it with a girl?"

Tim started to give a very exact answer to that, but he wasn't waiting for that. "You know I'm not putting it down. I figure for everyone's fair pair. I'm just wondering how it started is all. Was it something went wrong with a girl? Or what?"

"It's how I am," Tim told him. "It's what I am."

He knew what was called for, though—if it was in you, you'd have known it by this time, if it was coming out, it would have shown itself by now. People can be all sorts of things, do all kinds of things, without it affecting what you basically are.

"I just can't figure it," the young guy said, and went back down the hill shaking his head.

Still, it wasn't a response Tim minded necessarily, as

responses go, himself as the exceptional, the unprecedented encounter, the gratification of such basic requirements, the craftmanship of gratification, his own special satisfaction. He walked taller now, up the hill and across the gardens, where the same three figures were still situated

cho-cho-chuckala
with a rink-link-rucklaba

over the crest of the ridge, the tips of the downtown buildings just visible above the top of the next hill, half the width and half the height of its plane, and that half again the width and slant of the slope spread out below him, the silhouette of the clubhouse on his right matched with some shrubbery on his left, a tree a little past that with two smaller trees a little farther down on the other side, mass for line, ground with sky, his steps in perfect pace with the evening.

Esther's return prefigured a series of changes in the club, most of them coinciding with the close of the school term, when the three university clubs telescoped down to one to practice together for the summer. The third weekend of May was spring special training, followed in ten days by the spring *qu* test, in which Oster and Little Eva again failed to receive blackbelts, after which came a series of yearend parties, opulent potluck spreads heavy on zucchini and bulgur, where everybody stood around flexing their fingers back and trading stories of favorite practices.

(About this same time, too, the move to federate the clubs necessitated the establishment of a permanent *dojo* in the city, which, once found, had to be cleared out, sanded down, and revarnished, and this in turn necessitated a closer affiliation with the black club, the one commercial, non-university branch of the school in the city, which resulted in some talk—though subdued, the university clubs having some of their own black members—that the clubs were being taken in by the blacks, the clubs providing the material and better part of the labor so that the blacks could have their own place to practice in their own part of the city. In short, a politics began to develop, which Tim, who cared no more about it than to avoid any impression of avoiding it, relished as yet another dimension in the underlying absurdity of the whole enterprise.)

Three days before the start of special training, Esther cut off the tip of her finger on a bandsaw, and was told by her doctor that she wouldn't be able to practice for at least three weeks.

"These things are brought to us," Tim suggested, "as a way of keeping us from taking our commitments too seriously"—but she failed to find any merit in that point of view.

In the summertime they practiced outdoors on the Tech lawn, a long grassy concourse set inside a neat symmetry of buildings and walks. At the lower end the lawn dropped off into a deep wooded ravine, on the far side of which rose three squat cylindrical towers, the A, B, and C dorms of the St. Vincent's campus, dubbed by the students Ajax, Babo, and Comet, and it was possible to chart the progress of the second hour of practice by the passage of the sun, nudging the upper righthand corner of the lefthand tower, down a steep trajectory to a point about a third of the way from the bottom of the center tower, to disappear, about the time they were finishing sparring and starting *kata*, into a blaze of amber refraction, the lawn for those final fifteen or twenty minutes a network of chartreuse highlights against a field of verdant black, the shadows of their maneuvers stretching fifty, sixty yards, almost to the row of hedges that ran across the front of the porch of the Architecture Building.

Tim hated it, though. However deserted the campus might be, there was always a steady stream of stragglers filing by, each one of which invariably had to stop and ponder and point. He had living room muscles, calisthenics muscles, a thick trunk and arms and then spindle legs and something of a paunch. Moreover he always sweat a lot. Even before warm-ups were through, his *gi* would be marked down the back with damp spots, and after every sequence he'd be having to be pulling up and retying. One night a little black kid's dog, excited by all the shouting, bit him on the back of the thigh.

A week before special training, a couple of weeks after Esther had returned, another former member, a blackbelt named Paul, came back to the club after two years in the army, where he'd been stationed in Salt Lake City, and for a time had trained at the central *dojo* in Oakland.

(It intrigued Tim, once he discovered they had both started in the same beginners' group, had left the club at around the same time, and now were returning within a couple of weeks of each other, how little apparent attention they paid each other; at first he thought it was some buried competitiveness, a case of some long-standing antagonism, but there was no real evidence of that, their dealings were all cordial, just uninterested; rather, he decided finally, a typical example of like oblivious to like.)

Paul was around twenty-four, not tall, about five-eight or five-nine, with straw blond hair cropped close and parted straight back the side, the army looked superimposed over a face that was basically boyish and fair, apple cheeks, a few light speckles of beard dotting the moustache line and around the point of the chin—all of which made the ferocity of his approach that much more intimidating. At first Tim thought he was only extending himself as a way of regratiating himself back into the group, or of setting an example for special training, but after a week after special training had gone by, after two and then three weeks had gone by, and after he heard that it wasn't after he got out of the army that he'd trained in Oakland, but while he was still stationed in Salt Lake City, driving 500 miles each way every weekend to sleep on the bare floor of the practice room, he knew he was in the presence of a true believer.

The first of June Emil left to work for 3M in Connecticut for the summer, and Paul took over the Tuesday night practice. June was muggy and hot, and around the middle of the month there was a four-day stagnation alert. "Take it little easy tonight," Paul would tell them, "air's bad tonight, work more for form than strength tonight"—but so provocative were these words leaving his lips, so anathema even the idea of giving anything less than the fullest effort, that before the first half hour was out he was calling for deeper punches, higher kicks—"Faster! Harder!"—the brownbelts at his instigation going around with their belts off, swatting ass—"Lower there! Try there!"

Tim stopped going to Tuesday night practice. He'd been having trouble with his knees in February and March, with the wrap bandages and the needles into the kneecaps. He started spending Tuesday evening on the living room floor, the same span of time, the full two hours, stretching, limbering, form-building exercises.

By this time, though, Paul's spirit had so permeated the club that it colored even those practices he didn't personally lead. Here the ethic was to extend yourself, to push beyond your capabilities. By ignoring the pain of your body, you overcame your weakness, by being master over yourself, you became master over your opponent. He simply stood for the established creed.

"Suppose you're standing at the bus stop some night," Paul would tell them at the end of a practice, "you're walking down a dark alley and five guys jump you"—throwing little grins back over his shoulder, as if to choruses of accolades called to him from the shrubbery and the trees.

It was a function, finally, of it being summertime. Emil was away, Dietz was away, for the last two weeks of June Esther was in Nova Scotia, Ed Able was busy getting married, the brownbelts were in a rapture of dedication anyway. Amoto, who made a career of inscrutability, also made a career of letting things go by him.

110

One night he saw him kick Sominex, who nobody else even bothered with anymore, just casually as he was going by him, like you'd kick a piece of cardboard out of your way on the street.

"You kicked him," Tim said.

"No talking in line. Down there."

"You kicked him. You kick your students?"

"He was cheating. Mr. Shuri kicks his students when they don't try hard enough. No talking in line"—with three quick maneuvers he circled around Tim, swatting shoulder, rump, thigh—"Lower stance! Down there! Try there!"—and continued on down the line.

Cheating—it was a moral issue with him. What Tim thought afterward that he should have told him was that a gentleman doesn't need coercion to lead, a gentleman leads by quiet persuasion and example. But he could see a direct confrontation wasn't going to be the way to deal with him.

For the final fifteen or twenty minutes they did *kata*, ritualized combat routines designed for countering four, six, or eight opponents, three lines of eight spread across the grass, each member in turn counting out the steps. Most of the others counted in Japanese, *"Ich...nee...sun...chee...,"* but Tim considered this an affectation.

"One...two..."

"Louder."

"Three..."

"More forceful, louder."

Tim stopped counting.

"You put into your voice the force you expect your body to show. Go through again." Paul was at the end of the first row facing front, and hadn't yet looked around.

Timing his pause, Tim said, "I don't understand. You'll have to show me."

Without a moment's hesitation, Paul was around and back through the lines, "You put into your voice," gave Tim a shove hard with both hands against the chest, sending him back a step or two, "the spirit you want the others to show in their movements," turned and walked back to place. "Go through again."

That was the last time for three weeks Tim went to practice. He counted through again, no louder really than before, and this might have been seen as having held his ground, and at the end neglected to give the command *yasume* to return to natural stance, which might be construed as a further act of defiance, though the fact was he'd simply forgot. He spent some considerable time afterward thinking through all he might have done or might have said—while feeling pretty much that the fact that he was thinking this much about it at all was reason in itself to be pulling back for a while.

It was not, he felt fairly convinced, any added element here, any case of the repressed impulse acting itself out as aggression. No Prussian officers hiding here. Paul was attractive, insofar as peak conditioning and an unassailable self-esteem in the prime of life could make any man attractive, though a little too clipped, a bit too close-chiselled for Tim's taste. It was in fact because he felt free of any motive in the case that he felt free in challenging him at all—at the same time recognizing that any move he made at this point would have to be construed as a challenge, that to opposing him there was no alternative except to be pulling back.

Lacking the customary male incentives, he lacked too the traditional masculine regard for stamina and will, and with it, any feeling of shame at not doing any more than he absolutely cared to do. Knowing perhaps better than any of them here the practical value of these skills—the virtue, for instance, of knowing how to deal with four or six opponents in a tight place—he valued still more his own right of choice, the right to choose the exact extent and nature of his commitment. It was a matter, simply, of whether he could let himself be pushed.

There was more certainly to it than that, and he did see

that nevertheless he would be backing down, and that there might be consequences to that more debilitating, more over-riding finally than any action he might take, but it was because he did see that that he saw the futility of taking any action at all. Driving through Singer Oval one afternoon, he spotted Paul ahead of him on his motorcycle, stopped at a red light. He was over a lane and right up to the light, his *gi* strapped in a tight, anonymous bundle on the rack behind him. It was Wednesday, Tim remembered there was a special blackbelt practice on Wednesday afternoons, and for as long as they sat there, for maybe a full half minute, he never looked around or saw Tim, and the moment the light changed started immediately up, looking neither right nor left—and it occurred to Tim that he wouldn't see, that in his mind there was probably no antagonism even existing. So confident was he of the integrity of his every move, that he would interpret any opposition merely as a sign of weakness, and out of tolerance, perhaps, out of his own idea of gener-osity, simply overlook it.

He set out as soon as it was getting dark, coming in on the river road through Elco, a swing around Riverside Park and past the Elco bluffs, where sometimes hitchhikers stood along the catch-fences hunting rides out to the dance bars in Dithridge and Clarksville. It was the Sunday after Fourth of July. The Fourth had fallen on a Tuesday this year, at the pinnacle of a week of mild and cloudless days, but three or four days ago the weather had turned hot, and the air started piling up and piling up until now it was a tangible factor in all transactions, shrouding any object larger than a fire hydrant in a stale grayish mist, blurring the lines of movement—through the market strip, where the forklift operators were working barechested tonight, a right on Calley and down Carlson a couple of blocks onto the Eight, a diagonal overlap-ping of two long rectangles of blocks looping the bus station

113

at one end and Schwabb Park at the other, with the lower end of Alliance and part of Ninth forming the long-bar, and two or three blocks along the river end of Oriel the crossbar, across Alliance and up Liting past the two churches and around the park, with an optional cut down the alleyway back of the Sholes, and then back down Philadelphia and the upper end of Alliance, a circuit of maybe twenty or twenty-five blocks in all.

On the newspaper stand at Philadelphia and Alliance two guys with their shirts off and beer cans in their hands were harassing the traffic, and it was a sign of the evening that there were some who were taking this for an invitation, and were slowing down, and hurriedly turning around for another pass by.

In the doorway of Guiding Light the Elastic Trick, a tall, scrawny, unattractive kid, so named for his propensity to mold into whatever contour he leaned against, who he didn't think anyone ever picked up, was standing horribly beaten and bandaged, the whole left side of his face swollen and discolored, but still out at his accustomed spot as usual, as if in warning, as if in some obscure form of reproach.

At Ninth and Philadelphia the man next to him at the light was rubbernecking all around—though at what or after what he wasn't sure. A good part of this same route was shared by the downtown hookers and their trade, and at two or three points crossed the stadium and the Hoit Hall traffic, and this time of night there was always a line of cars along the farther side of the park waiting for the bookkeeping shift at Dollar Bank to let out, and it was one of his recurring fantasies of these travels that he might one night make a chance turn and lock in with one of these, end up in some new part of the city with a new life, new habits and drives.

As he drove along he caught, as he frequently did, a perceptual tic, certain dominant features, certain doorways and sections of block standing out, like a stage set made up from a few representative props, or more, like a computer-enhancement in which all background irrelevancies have been bleeded out. For a long time he'd been hearing people talk about Pancherello's, going down to Da Paunch, and always wondered where this Pancherello's was, until one night he found out it was on Alliance next to where he would have had to go by it probably a hundred different times, and it was another one of his recurring fantasies that he passed over these routes invisible, a life that left no tracks, a foolish, and he knew, finally just careless point of view.

For a while he followed a stationwagon with the license I-DAD–#1 dad?—and then another one with a bumper sticker that read HELP ENSHRINE USS LAFFEY DD 729. He cut down the alleyway back of the bus station, where sometimes under the streetlights at the little cross-streets that connected to Oriel there would be somebody waiting, or along the fence that ran around the bus lot. These were the badlands now, a dismantled badlands, tucked into three or four vacant lots, a row of loading docks at the rear of three or four adjacent buildings, the field of derelict boxcars on the other side of the bus lot. There was a gap between the two fences just wide enough to squeeze through ("No chubbies, please," somebody had written down the side of one of the poles in fingernail polish), and one by one the last summer the cars had been broken into, until there had been one point in August it had been possible to walk across boards spread between the doorways of five of these, with a short leap into the sixth, into an absolute blackness where you'd never know what you might encounter, or had encountered. Coming back from here one night, he had met a skinny black man standing at the opening with a knife in his hand, and just shifted a little to one side, his feet a shoulder width apart and hands open and out a little from his sides, looked straight at him and said, "You come at me holding that knife, best you be sure that knife isn't holding onto you"—and it'd worked, either that had been too complicated for him to comprehend, or he'd comprehended it well enough, because he didn't

115

make a move, just stood there as if he was under an enchant-
ment, while Tim edged around him and out the opening.

But tonight there was nobody there, nobody on the
steps of the two churches on Liting, no one on the wall in
front of the bus station pretending to be between buses.

A bell jangled on the door as you came in. The movie
houses on Alliance were newer and better attended, but he
preferred this one on the tag end of Litchfield just after it
turned one-way, where you could be stopping off on your
way back from the bars in Dockside, on your way back to
your car.

There was nobody behind the change counter, and inside all the lights were on, the booths were being swept out—
Tim turned around and walked back out again. With the
blacklights on these places had a kind of gutter romanticism
that was almost appealing, but with real lights on it was
totally impossible.

He walked up to the corner and down the other side of
the street, pausing to examine the store windows. Every so
often somebody would come by and stop outside the theater,
as if trying to figure out what this could be, and then, with a
kind of investigative resolve, march on inside, or go a few
steps by and then suddenly, as if an invisible giant hand had
reached out and plucked them up, wheel around and dart
inside.

He waited about ten minutes and then went back inside.
The blacklights were on now, the coin man back behind his
counter, the doorbell jingled as he came through the door.
You entered through a small foyer done all in red and black,
red shag carpet and red flock wallpaper, and a pair of black
leatherette couches, the change counter a basement bar with
alternating diamonds of red and black—"Her," the counter
man was saying to somebody on the phone, "I wouldn't fuck
her with your dick"—through a bead curtain into a long,
high-ceilinged room that might at one time have been an
actual theater: the walls were needlessly high, almost as high

116

again as the height of the booths, and up near the ceiling on the farther wall were a couple of what looked like projection slots; walls, ceiling, the ducts and pipes running along the ceiling all painted black, the floor black tile. Whatever the broom had swept up had left a few damp stains up the middle of the aisle.

Four of the booths had lights on, and Tim stood sorting through his change until their occupants emerged, two of them men he'd seen come in while he was standing outside, and a businessman type with an attache case and a newspaper folded up under his arm, and then a pudgy black kid who took a slow time deliberating between booths, and after two or three went on out the door.

The doorbell jingled, and Dubonnet, who he'd known from the old Troy Hill days when he first came to town, walked in all smiles, in white shoes and a pair of light pants that showed butter yellow under the blacklights.

"How do?"

"How do."

He went around and checked the peepholes, then came over and joined Tim.

"Aren't we looking spiffy this evening," Tim told him.

Bonnie, pleased, went into a little flurry of revelations, "I was having dinner over at my sister's and we were having stuffed pork chops, and um-*um* I-want-to-tell-you, and they were all sitting down to play cards but I was feeling kinna sleepy, so I thought I'd just stop off a minute here on my way home, what is it, dead?"

"Dead," Tim nodded.

"It was dead the other night in here. They're all going up now to that new place on Gower, you know the one with the double booths and the cushion seats, you been up there yet?"

Tim hadn't.

"Um-*um*. This in here anymore, you know the other night in here some guy jumps out of the booth at Ron while

117

he's coming around checking the booths, slugs him on the head with a pipe rolled up in a newspaper, and runs out the door. And cops in here, maybe you noticed those two in the stationwagon along the side of the building when you came in, that's why I never come in here anymore."

This came out in bits while he was strolling up and down the aisle, but when he saw that Tim wasn't going to be encouraged to leave, he settled down beside him.

"It's dead."

"Dead," Tim nodded.

"Oh, then. And have you seen this new one they have now with the battery that goes inside your pocket, and when you get wet, the current—"

"Shocking," Tim said.

The doorbell jingled, and they separated and drifted down to opposite ends of the aisle. The curtain parted and a young kid with a wispy moustache walked in, not bad but a little soft looking, with a giveaway fussiness—looking all around, like he'd always wondered what one of these places could be like.

"It's dead."

"Dead."

"Last week I'm driving home from here, and I see these two young guys, well, you know I don't usually stop for a hitchhiker, least of all when there's two at a time, but these ones were dressed nice, though you could tell they'd been drinking—"

His fingers fluttered around the corners of his mouth, the nails with their clear lacquer yellow and luminous in the blacklight.

"And this one says to me, You mind if we light this joint? And I say, Go right ahead, as a matter of fact I might even try some myself, and the one that's in back kind of has his knee up against the back of the seat, so that when I reach back with the joint I figure if he doesn't—"

The doorbell jingled, and a middle-aged man wearing a

slicker raincoat buttoned to his neck came in carrying a shopping bag. Tim had wandered down to the far end of the aisle,
and as he was turning to walk back, the young kid, who he'd
almost forgotten about, motioned to him from inside the
doorway of one of the booths. He moved aside to let Tim
past him, easing up onto the stool and leaning back until his
head came to rest against the wall. He dropped a quarter into
the slot.

A black plumber working under the sink in coveralls was
being pestered by a negligeed housewife. He was only trying
to do his job, but she just wouldn't leave him be. The young
kid edged in to get a closer look.

"Where're you from?" he asked Tim.

"Ah, Spillway, Spillway." Tim slipped his hand around
the back of his neck, tracing a fingertip along his hair line.

"And did you go to school in Spillway?"

"School in Spillway? Ah, yeah, yeah, school in
Spillway."

"And when you were in school, did you ever play
hookey from school?"

About this time Tim started to remember he'd met this
particular kid before.

"And when you played hookey from school, and you
got caught, what did they do to you?"

"Scusez."

Tim squeezed by him and back out of the booth, and a
minute later, when he emerged and walked by Tim, neither
of them showed the least sign of recognition.

Dubonnet was gone now, or inside one of the booths,
and the Segar had come in, an imposing looking black man
with muttonchop whiskers who was his postman by day but
by night appeared here in three-piece suits with a big cigar
that he went around from booth to booth puffing on like a
dog pissing on every tree.

The doorbell jingled and an incredibly tall, incredibly
skinny, incredibly black boy in scarlet basketball silks and

stripe-matched socks and one of these strap-on beaks that all the black queens were liking this year walked in, walked all the way down to the end of the aisle, turned around, and walked back out again, followed almost immediately by another, shorter, very muscular, and equally dark number in skin-close white jeans and a white temptation top, who did likewise. It was show night tonight. Up at the head of the aisle an old man was standing coughing, and had maybe been standing coughing for as long as he'd been there, single, dry, dislocated coughs, one every ten or fifteen seconds, while the man in the slicker raincoat, who had what looked like three or four more coats buttoned up underneath that, was going around very conscientiously reading all the signs, and munching on something crunchy that he had to dig around for in the bottom of his bag.

The signs were of three varieties: commercial blacklight posters tacked up around the walls just under the ceiling, cosmic spacegirls and copulating abstracts; next to the doors of the booths one or two small denominational signs, 2BOYS 1GIRL, TWO+ONE=FUN, FUN WITH BLACK & WHITE; and accompanying these, handpainted title signs that Arthur the nightshift man made, BIG BANANA and MAGIC MOUTHS, HUMAN SANDWICH subtitled DOUBLE JOINTED, BAR TEND HER and COCKTAILS FOR TWO, COCK and TAILS in different colored letters, with little beds and WOW signs painted in the corners. These last apparently were thought to have talismanic powers, because there were as many as nine and ten of them tacked around some of the doors. He was leaning against the side of one of the booths picking at the corner of one of these, and as the doorbell jingled just lifted his head, as Paul came through the curtain.

Just inside he paused, and there was a second or two before his eyes started to pick out details, where Tim could have slipped inside one of the booths and been passed by unseen, and that he didn't afterwards had to seem, in however dim a way, to have been deliberate.

"What's good in here, anything?"

"There's a couple over here that aren't bad, this one here was okay—want to try one?"

"No, that's all right, I was just seeing what it's like"— and he turned and walked back out the door.

Tim was right behind him. He hadn't meant to make a move, rather the opportunity not to make a move, to turn the encounter casual and unmemorable, but he immediately saw that if he left it at this it could only have an opposite effect; so in each step that followed was the crucial thing to avoid the break coming at that particular point, and the only way of avoiding that to push ahead to the next possible step.

Outside the door Paul turned left, Tim alongside him now, and started up the block, neither of them looking at each other or saying a word, not matching each other exactly, they weren't moving in step, for example, but at a pace too rapid for nonchalance—up ahead he saw a man coming the other way shift out toward the curb. At the corner they both swung another left, and immediately around the corner Paul's motorcycle was parked, and directly in front of it was Tim's car. He hadn't identified the car as Tim's, and betrayed some surprise when Tim walked over and unlocked it.

Tim smiled blandly and said, "Looks like our paths are crossed this evening."

Paul nodded, more of a shrug than a nod, and said something about having just come back from the Blue Marble— "except you know that's really just a neighborhood bar."

Tim said, "I was just going to say maybe you'd care to stop off and have a beer."

"You know some places around here that are good?"

"Probably this late on a Sunday night there might not be too many open. But I have some back at my place, we could stop off there."

Paul had been fitting on his helmet, but now he took it off again and held it under his arm while he deliberated. He was a person who would always give that second or two of consideration to any question he was asked, however trivial. He had a way when he was being serious of pulling down the corners of his mouth and looking over to the side—that was the look he'd wear at thirty or thirty-five. That's the way our faces change, Tim was thinking, the way we form our faces as much as our faces form us.

Or he'd grow out of it, maybe, grow into his authority, more trusting of the immediacy of his own responses.

"You go on, I'll follow you."

It was a fifteen- or twenty-minute drive, across the broad end of downtown and up the Streets Run through a long succession of lights, at each intersection having to slow down and check back, Paul lagging perpetually behind, until after a while he stopped worrying about him, for long stretches almost forgetting he was back there, thinking no more about it than to think that whatever happenstance would bring him, happenstance was guaranteed to make right.

Then when they reached the house, as he was kicking down his stands and pulling off his gloves, Paul pointed over the rooftops in the direction of Wilmer, which was only a couple of blocks away, and said, "Twenty-two months ago, and I'd have been sitting over there in one of those desks."

"Twenty-two months? How old are you now?"

"I'll be twenty-one in twenty-three more days. I'm in one of these new forty-nine-month programs, where they have you in for seven months and then you're out for seven months, and the government pays for your training. I start an internship down at Rolinar tomorrow morning."

Immediately Tim's whole impression of him changed— his actual appearance seemed to change—what had seemed the man's too-earnest self-regard revealing itself as the promising boy's tight-held apprehension at not being taken entirely seriously.

Climbing the walk, mounting the steps to the porch, his

eyes were constantly in motion, measuring, checking out. Though still fairly young, he carried in him already the habits of a man of knowledge. He would never walk into any place where danger waited him.

Tim bustled ahead of him—"I've had this place for almost two years now, I used to have another place up on Sussman that was bigger than this, I've had three places since I've lived in the city. This one is really only two rooms, but they're on two different floors, so you don't really feel it's such a tiny place. It's a two-room duplex, you know?"

Inside the door Paul picked up and dropped one foot and then the other, the remnant of some wintertime stomping gesture, looked around, and said, "Hey, nice place."

"What can I offer you? Beer? Juice? Something stronger?"

"What d'you have?"

"I have apple juice, grapefruit juice, sorry no orange juice. Bourbon, scotch, a little tequila. Vodka with tonic, white wine. Encino."

"Bourbon's fine for me. Ice, little water."

He went over and sat down on the couch. Tim mixed him his drink and took it over—he was sitting hunched up on the edge of the couch, and reached up to take the glass without lifting his head—and then went around and did the things he did, lit a couple candles, lit a stick of incense and stuck it into one of the plant pots, put a record on, and as he was passing the couch noticed that Paul's glass was almost empty and offered him a refill, which he accepted. Then he made a quick trip upstairs, and apparently that was a mistake, because when he came back down and sat down on the couch next to him, he was all clenched up, and his glass was already two-thirds of the way empty, and what he thought was there was something that was bothering him, he'd come here with something on his mind and maybe he could help.

"Is something the matter?" Tim asked him. "Is there anything I can do?"

This triggered off an excited and jumbled response—
"Now, I don't want you to think I've been jagging you"—
jumping up and immediately sitting back down again—"don't
mean to be, don't want you to think I'd be jagging you"—the
gist of it being that when he'd heard Tim ask him over, what
he heard was himself asking girls the same question.

"Well," Tim said, "you never know what'll bring 'em."

Paul leapt to his feet and started pacing the floor, "My
mind's not straight, I've had these drinks, I can't make decisions when my mind's not straight, I've got to have time and
think this over, I'm not trying to jag you, though."

"Don't mean to be jagging you," he kept saying. What
he was saying was, I'm getting out of here.

"But I don't want you to think I've been jagging you."

"Wait a minute, wait, wait, wait a minute now, just
wait a minute here, what're you saying, you're saying you're
walking out of here now?"

"My mind's not straight, I can't make these decisions
while my mind's not straight, I've had these couple of drinks,
I've got to have some time to think this over."

"All right, all right, now, let's just slow down here a
minute now."

They were both on their feet now, circling each other
around the middle of the floor. At a certain point Tim could
feel him drawing into himself, consciously taking command
of himself, a watchful and then inquisitive look coming into
his eyes.

He gave Tim a sidelong look and said, "Do you always
talk like that? Take a line like that?"

"Oh, yeah, the quick lip, yeah, yeah, story of my life
right there."

"I mean take a line with someone like that."

"Oh. Well. Well, see—you see, you put something out in
front of somebody, and see how they react. As a way of
finding out what they are."

Paul nodded. He'd only been interested in how it

worked.

"Don't you like women at all?" was the next thing he wanted to know.

"I wouldn't put it like that," Tim said.

"I'm not putting it down, you understand. Was it something that went wrong with a woman? Or have you always been that way?"

"It's my nature," Tim told him. "It's what I am."

From that point on though he could see there would be no getting through to him at all. Still there was the actual business of getting him out the door, Paul wanting to recount some incidents that had happened to him hitchhiking in the desert in Utah and Nevada, and then to leave on the note that he was only going to think things over and maybe later on would be back to talk some more, Tim going over to the end of the couch sitting with his knees drawn up, going "I see, yes, that's right," and "No, no, that's all right, no, that's all right"—until suddenly he just turned and bolted out the door, an abrupt, awkward parting.

For a long time he didn't make a move, but just sat where he was, on the couch. He'd been there at the most fifteen, maybe twenty minutes. He'd left the door into the hall a little ajar, and he didn't think had fully secured the bottom door, either—leaving himself, if only symbolically, a way back in—and Tim knew he ought, as a first step toward putting this whole episode out of his mind, to go down and lock them, but for a long time he didn't, just sat, his mind empty and lax. He'd been through episodes like this before, situations where he'd supposed too much, where something he'd assumed to be tacit had later been withdrawn, and each time they left him the same way, drained, depleted of all reserves. Unmanned, he thought of it. He told himself that it was only a principle involved here, and not necessarily an indictment of himself personally, or alternately, was only personal, some error of approach, a misstep on his part, that needn't be read as an entire life judgment, and in any case he'd been honest, had concealed nothing.

Eventually he did go downstairs and locked up, climbed the stairs to the upper floor and undressed and turned down the bed, leaving the light on over the kitchen sink and the stairway light on, in case he should come back by looking to see a light, and even after he was in bed was still half listening —keeping alive as long as possible the possibility he might still be back and this cleared up, deferring as long as possible the official start of his unhappiness, on the chance that some of it might slip by him subliminally. He knew what was in store for him now. It was a two- or three-day process, in which he would have to rehearse back through line for line everything that had been said, or might have been said, or might still be said—for fairly early on he recognized that now he would have to start back to practice again, and that raised a whole new series of contingencies and doubts, so that it wasn't for another full week that he actually went back, and by then he'd been dead for nine days. He'd run his motorcycle off a turn on a back country road the other side of Clydedale, killed instantly. By this time, details had cooled, and interest shifted to more prodigious aspects, such as him having been killed "instantly," and having been just twenty-two days short of turning twenty-one, so that Tim was never sure afterward how he'd even determined it was that same night it had happened. He was in the locker room getting dressed for practice, and Mike Houser was describing how he'd driven over there the day before on his bike, and the dumpster, it was a dumpster he'd crashed into, wasn't even set straight but on an angle with the turn, and "if he'd been just fifteen degrees shorter, or fifteen degrees wider coming around there—"

He'd gone out that night in the state he was in and killed himself.

He'd killed him—and because he thought that first,

before he even knew any particulars of the case, always led him afterwards to feel that he could to some measure discount it in his mind.

At the same time he recognized that this was to be an event totally without consequence, that no connection was likely ever to be drawn to himself, that whatever penalties were to be extracted here were to be entirely out of his own mind.

His immediate thought was only to make it through practice, to show nothing, lining up, bowing in, running through warmups, having to follow the others to perform the simplest of moves, down the floor and back, a turn and then back, slipping into a lulling of routine, an easing forgetfulness out of which each second he would have to encounter it, and the next second again fresh from the start—this was what shock is, he was thinking, the confrontation with the thing greater than our capacity to absorb it, so that we must re-encounter and re-encounter it full until the quota can be filled; crossing the floor and picking up his bag and down to the showers and out to his car, climbing the stairs to the upper floor, pausing to spread his *gi* out over the shower rod to dry, to settle down finally into the spot he'd reserved for himself in his mind, on the floor next to the window in the alcove off the bed.

It was nearly dark, only the water tower on top of the next hill and a low flat building next to it that might be either a hospital or a school all that was still distinguishable against the sky. The window swung in, coming between his back and the wall, so that he had to lean in, his forehead against the sidebar of the frame, his hand gripping the sill. The feeling was of things moving very fast all around him, and he had to hold very tight, and keep very still, if he was to keep track of even a fraction of it all.

It was a thing that was unassailable, there was going to be this thing now in his life that he was going to have to deal with, that by its very nature he was going to have no way at all of being able to deal with. It was like a border he was unable to cross, or more properly a territory he was confined to, that no matter what direction he set out in he was unable to go more than a few steps before he was stumbling and faltering.

At some point in his life he'd come to realize that ordinary rules of conduct were inapplicable in his case, and had turned his back on them, wandering off the common path into an antinomian wilderness, a dark wood from which reason was no guide.

After around midnight the street began to quiet, and from then on each occasional arrival and stir along the block took on a disproportionate significance, the night becoming a perpetual series of accusations and alarms. Around four o'clock he went over and lay down on the bed, on his back with his knees drawn up and the heels of his hands pressed into his eyes, until around six, when he went back to the window to watch the water tower and the buildings around it take shape in the morning light, until it was time to get ready for work, and as soon as he returned home that evening returned to that same spot, to the window, giving himself over to a schedule of remorse, to certain designated postures and hours of the day (so much so that after three or four days the bar of the windowframe had printed a permanent crease across his forehead, and several people remarked on it), giving himself over, almost unwittingly, to endurance, to recovery, to—as he came increasingly to feel it—a blunting, a smoothing over, a compromise, cutting himself off from his ordinary ties and obligations and noting, not for the first time, how easy it is to lapse into the background, how widely our lives may veer, and nobody even notice.

One of the curious aspects of the thing for him was a peripheral sharpening—of vision, feeling—for the play of light on the bricks of the sidestreet below, for subtle variations in the changing aspect of the water tower against the sky, as if all the emotion were being squeezed out around the edges. At work he was more deliberate, more painstaking, his judgments surer and more rapidly formed, at practice (for through all of this he continued diligently to attend practice) he felt himself coming nearer the stance, his concentration sharper, his endurance lengthened. After a week or ten days had gone by, he hadn't so much assimilated as exhausted the feeling, and from then on had to be especially on guard against some casual reference to it slipping out in conversation. At night he encountered it in grossly literal symbolizations in his dreams, giant pointing fingers and crowds that turned their backs on him in the street.

And at times a bitter hilarity seized him—for what was he to think, finally, that so repugnant was his love, that even the thought of it was enough to drive strong men to their deaths?

One night as he was coming down the steps after practice, he heard Burger King, one of the St. Vincent brownbelts, talking about going down to Tantoni's with Paul after practice and shooting burners, more of an intonation than any actual remark, but enough to send him on a chance to Ed Able.

He said, "That's a little unusual, isn't it, a blackbelt and a drinker?"—and saw from the response the extent to which this was true.

"There was never anyone more dedicated than Paul Hough," Ed Able told him. "Paul and I used to live on Frew Street together, and three or four in the morning sometimes, if we couldn't get to sleep, we'd get up and do two or three hundred front kicks together—"

After that Tim started sorting back through again, certain inconsistencies he'd let slip by him before, those five-hundred-mile every weekend drives, and the strange intensity of his whole style. So maybe their paths had been more than crossed that evening after all. If so, it wouldn't be the first time he'd borne the burden of another man's demon.

Those three and four a.m. kicking sessions were especially revealing, the two of them tossing on their respective pillows. *Hey, Ed. Huhn? Hey, wanna do some front kicks?*

After a while he began to feel even angry over it, seeing that whatever the case, it was going to have its change on him anyway, coming in the end to feel, as he had so many occasions earlier in his life, himself the victim of the affair.

He was lying downstairs on the couch, his arms hanging back over the arm. There had been a shower of sunspots playing over the top of the coffee table and the back of the couch when he first lay down, but now, though an impression of daylight was still hanging in the air, all around the surfaces of the room were black. He scooped up his wallet and keys, turned over some papers that had been lying out on the coffee table—the buzzer sounded twice more before he could reach the bottom of the stairs. He pulled aside the curtain, and saw Esther Hardy standing outside. She had moved a couple of steps back from the door and was looking away to one side. She'd never been here before, and he hadn't even known had known where he lived, but different times they'd talked, and a couple of times had gone out to eat with some other people after practice, and he wasn't entirely surprised to find her here now.

"I didn't see any light on, I was afraid you probably weren't going to be here."

"Oh, no, no, not at all, in fact I'm glad you rang, I sleep this early and then I can't get any sleep later on. Can I offer you something? I have wine, I could heat water for instant coffee or tea, I have apple juice, grapefruit juice."

"No, just apple juice's fine for me."

First she had to go around and comment on everything. She had a wide, bright, wondering gaze, and listened carefully to everything that was said to her. A bit of this came over as slow-wittedness, a kind of warrior pose—the buffoon manqué —the male counterpart of which he'd encountered various times in the past. She was wearing loose pleated pants, belled all the way up like a *gi*, and a loose sleeveless sweater. A narrow stripe of suntan ran the length of the back of her arms, arms that were long and uniformly thin, the wrists disconcertingly frail. Her hair was parted down the center and pinned behind the ears in a practical style, emphasizing still more the wideness and directness of her gaze. She was right to emphasize the eyes, they were fine, clear, untroubled eyes, a pale gray with tiny chips of amber and deeper gray sprinkled around the pupils.

She sat on a low hassock, smiling and rolling a glass of apple juice on her knee.

"So, and you live all alone here?"

"Oh, yes, all alone."

"That must get lonely sometimes, I imagine you'd get very lonely here sometimes."

"Oh, well, but you know everybody's got to find their own way."

She nodded, examined something on her left, something on her right.

She said, "You know, I've been watching you lately at practice."

"Oh? You think I show any future?"

She had to think a minute about that.

"You're not bad. There are ways you could be very good. There are things you have that you could build on."

He'd found on these occasions that a direct declaration is always best, that the less angling is done early on, the better the chances later for an accommodation.

He said, "You know, I probably ought to tell you, I'm strictly one of the guys."

"What does that mean?"

"It means I'm gay."

She said, "I thought probably you might be. That was one of the things I wanted to find out."

He waited to see where she would take this now.

131

"You know, I actually live very close to here, on the top of Castlemaine near Dobbs. I go by here when I'm going to pick up my lumber, though I doubt if you've ever noticed me in my van."

Still he was waiting to see where she was going with this.

"One of the funny things, I felt, one of the things that always stuck out with me about Paul and me in the club, is while we had almost the same history in the club, we started in the same beginner group, and left the club almost at the same time, and were away almost exactly the same time, we even returned with some of the same moves—we were never really friends. Though I always felt there was some special understanding that we had, like there were things about him that I could know that nobody else would ever know, and vice versa."

In a way he was almost relieved. He'd gone into the kitchen section to put on water or take something out of the refrigerator, but now came back and sat down on the couch facing her, leaning in until his eyes were level with her own.

"I can't know," he said to her, "I can't ever say for certain what extent something I might have said, something he could have interpreted out of anything that happened here might have contributed to what he did that night, but I am certain. That nothing I intentionally said, nothing that could have happened here in any way outright figured, on that much I am sure."

She gazed at him unjudgingly, saying nothing.

"I don't know to what extent I'm the contributor to, was only the bystander of what was going on inside him, I think in all honesty fairly little. I've asked myself the hard questions that I can, and I don't believe that I am. I don't in any honesty feel that I am."

"But you have these doubts," she said.

"I think I'll always have doubts, and pay a penalty as high for them as if I were to be sure. But I don't believe that I am. As far as I can ever know, as truly as I can ever feel, I don't believe I am.''

"But still you have these doubts.''

"I have these doubts—if I didn't have doubts, if I was positive, wouldn't that tell you something there? What better answer could I give you?''

He didn't quite catch what she said to that.

"You're heavier," she said, "but I'm more advanced. My speed up against your strength. We're about even matched.''

"You want to fight me?''

"In overcoming me, you overcome my suspicions, and vanish your own doubts. Though neither of us can know the truth, the truth will make one or the other of us stronger.''

A second or two went by in which he tried to gauge just how serious she might be—and in which he wasn't fully able to repress a smile.

"We'll go over to the new *dojo*. I have a key.''

"I just have to get my *gi*.''

He'd left the *gi* over the shower rod to dry, and first it would have to be ironed. He didn't have a proper ironing board, and had to clear off one of the tables to use instead. He never quite got around to putting things away, and there were piles of canned goods and packages of light bulbs scattered over the furniture, and little stacks of magazines and correspondence planted around the floor. She shifted back into the easy chair, relocating onto the floor a pile of new, variously colored socks on top of a crumpled store bag that had been sitting on the arm.

He started rinsing out some dishes, "I don't like to leave my place unless everything's just the way I want it.''

She nodded, "I must spend twenty minutes on my bench before I start in the morning, and again before I walk away at night.''

He wiped the sink, did some business with the blinds, straightened out a few things on the shelves, all the time keeping up a running dissertation on the virtues of steam cooking, "It's only lately I've been doing almost all my cooking by steamer. It keeps in flavor and cuts vitamin loss. You know, you can cook more ears if you steam your corn instead of boil it, plus you eliminate the danger of splashing. Or squash, I wash 'em, scrape 'em, slice, sprinkle with a little white pepper and grated parmesan cheese. And string beans. And dry fruit—you can save the liquid for a brew with a little brown sugar and powdered cloves."

She nodded, taking it all in, showing no impatience. She was giving her evening to this.

"How do you feel about women, then?" she finally asked.

"Women, then?"

"You were saying you go for guys, how do you feel about women, then?"

"I like women." He came back over and sat on the couch. "I don't dislike women, or resent women. I don't see myself in any kind of competition with a woman. I think I have an understanding of the kind of conflicts a woman has to deal with, conflicts that probably she is prepared more efficiently to resolve."

"And have you always felt like this? Was there ever a—"

"Actually," Tim said, "actually I think it's the thing I lack that I crave, the essence of a man. Something of a transsubstantiation idea in that for sure. In a way, I think it's a way of making myself more a man." The forthrightness of this he could see was going a long way toward turning her around, and he wasn't able to resist adding: "Actually, I think it's probably even more quantitative than that, a certain quota—a certain yardage I feel I have to cover each month."

It took her a second or two for the implications of this to begin to settle in, and then he could feel her straightening up in her chair; he could see that as usual he would be paying high dividends for scoring these points. Now she was only waiting for him. After a couple more minutes of stalling, he gathered up his *gi* and stuffed it into his bag, and said, "All set!"

Her van was parked out front, a big, anonymous-looking Dodge van painted telephone-truck green. She opened up the back for him to see inside—a complete living unit, kitchenette, bunk bed, a table with two fold-down chairs, the joints so painstakingly worked they seemed to be budding from the grain. "This has two burners, this is insulated but not refrigerated, I believe if you're going to be more than two days away from processed foods, you'd best be prepared to live off the land, this folds down, this opens out." Fire extinguisher, flares, tools and sundries behind the side panels, blankets, towels, and clothing in tight tubular bundles in back of the ceiling slats—"for added insulation"—a drop-down ironing board that locked into a slot on the back of one of the chairs, even a tiny aquarium built into one wall, all surprisingly frilly and feminine, the bedspread, curtains, and tablecloth a matched gingham check. Her manner, too, was softer now, more easygoing. He realized she'd taken all that business upstairs as confessional, and this was her way of returning it.

"I'll drive over, you can follow me."

The new *dojo* was inside Singer Oval, a four-lane traffic bypass set down around the old east-end shopping district, marooning it from access on every side. After dark it was all but deserted in here, except for an occasional bewildered derelict, and a few scattered clumps of bus transfers, grouped tight together like vigils, the long rows of darkened shops, the broad stretches of mall paving, the three churches on one intersection with the rust-concept fountain in the middle, lighted by special crime-deterrent lamps, having the overclarification of a stage set, on which every actual encounter was made muddled and scary.

The *dojo* was above a florist's, in a tall green frame building that connected at the rear with a lower, longer gray-shingled building with a slanted roof and no windows. She let them in by a door almost at the end of the other building, leading the way up a steep flight of stairs and down a narrow hallway, and then up four more steps to another locked door, not putting on any lights—"There'll be enough light from the windows once we get inside to see by." It occurred to him she must come here regularly, probably every night like this.

They came in the back way, picking their way down a long hallway past stacks of plasterboard and big cans of something, past a couple of small offices and two smaller practice rooms that had been partitioned out of a larger space, through a curtained doorway into the *dojo* proper, a wide, high-ceilinged room with bare varnished floors and rows of high windows across the left and front walls, that let in, as promised, plenty of light to maneuver by. Around the sides of the room were areas of deep shadow, a pair of hanging ferns silhouetted above the sloping line of the partition, the right wall alternating mirrors with exercise bars. The floorboards were edged with fine lines of light, but inside the mirrors the floor was a solid dark space, blacker than black.

She put her bag down next to the partition and started undressing, fragments of silhouetted elbow and hunched-up back popping out and being quickly reabsorbed back into the darkness behind her. He took his bag over to the end of the row of mirrors and set it down. As she reached her arms back into her jacket, the light caught a bright keyboard of ribs, a narrow, practically flat chest. She was too thin, too tall, her center of gravity would be high, probably too high.

He'd just gotten a new *gi*, and it hadn't quite shrunk down yet. The belt was one of these new wear-resistant fabrics, that appeared to be knot-resistant as well.

She walked out to the middle of the floor, stretched and bent, brought her elbows then her head to the floor, tried a few practice kicks. He wandered around for a while, as if hunting for just the right place, pushed up onto tiptoes a couple of times, then bent down brushing his knuckles to the floor.

"We bow in."

They faced each other and brought their feet together,

bowing from the waist.

"*Ra.*"

"*Ra.*"

They started circling, easing in and out of stance, moving in a few steps, and then back, keeping always just a step or two outside of striking range, a quick thrust in, and then quickly back, in, and back, the slant of the partition, the silhouettes of the two hanging plants, the left wall of windows passing behind her, then the front wall, the right wall of mirrors, the curtained doorway, and back around to the partition again, the lower of the two plants momentarily situated behind her head like a fantastical bonnet—and it came as a distinct surprise as the first blow struck him, a quick jab to the solar plexus, and immediately she was back and out and circling, hips low, body turned, offering the narrowest possible target of retaliation.

He'd never been hit before. At practice the standard was to deliver the blow with maximum force to a point just short of contact. The two times he'd ever hit anyone himself, one time the Sominex wholly by accident, and once Ed Able in free spar after he'd had his guard down, he'd been let to feel it was tantamount to disgrace, fully half of the club coming up to him afterward to assure him he needn't feel badly about it. That blow was followed immediately by another a little lower, both of them quick, deliberate lunge punches.

He'd been knocked out of stance and taken a couple steps to the side, and as she came in again he continued his sideways movement another step or two, caught hold of her wrist and spun her around, as he let go giving her a side-thrust kick to the rump that sent her sprawling.

Then he went over and tried a technique that Emil had showed them one time, offering her a hand up saying, "Hey, you know you could hurt yourself doing that," and making a joke out of it. But either he'd kicked her too hard, or, as he was beginning more and more to suspect, she was just void of any sense of humor, because she came up with a side-snap kick to the groin that he just barely blocked, followed by a hard slap across the face.

Immediately she was back and out, circling, her eyes fixed on his—coming immediately back in with another lunge punch. He came up with a counterpunch, more a block than punch, that stopped just short of her nose.

"Don't hold back. Don't be holding back."

She moved in with another slap across the other side of his face, then quickly back and out, circled half around, and then back, her shield arm loose and bobbing, like teasing an invisible line.

"Come on. Come on."

Her movements were more economical now—as he made a thrust she moved only a single step aside, quickly returning in with another slap to the other side of his face, then taking only a step or two back, her breathing controlled, her eyes never varying from his own.

"Come on, come on."

A wearied melancholy began to spread over him, his face burning and streaming sweat, his eyes tearing. He moved toward the center of the floor—twice again she was in, with another slap and then a lunge punch, blows he more acknowledged than fended—taking a position at the center of the floor facing the left wall of windows, his head tilted back, his arms slack at his sides. He could never know if this punishment was merited, but perhaps the only way to lift himself of the burden of it was to endure it to the full.

"Come on."

He fixed his eyes on the second window from the front, on one of the lower spires of the nearer of the two churches, that had a crescent of rust-sculpture superimposed over its lower half.

"You have to fight me, come on."

She hit him with a side-thrust kick to the right buttock, knocking him momentarily out of stance. He repositioned his legs a little wider apart, knees slightly bent.

"You have to fight me, you have to fight me."

She gave him another side-thrust kick hard as she could directly from behind, this time failing to budge him, and then circled around front, pantomiming blows to his face, then gave him several hard slaps back and forth across his face, and then a sharp back-knuckle strike to each nipple, that made his *gi* crack.

"Come on, you have to fight me, come on, you have to fight me."

At a certain point he began to feel her bringing her anger under control. She was in back of him, had been aiming little nip-kicks at his buttocks and the backs of his thighs, and then for a minute or two there was a gradual slowing down, a barely discernible slackening of blows, and after that he could feel a pattern beginning to develop. She began to scatter her blows, aiming higher, to the shoulders and upper arms, tracing a jersey line along his collarbone, working exclusively with side-snap and roundhouse kicks now, quick, sharp strikes with the stinging edge of the foot, moving around his body in a generally counterclockwise and downward progression to a point just below the knees, a blow to the right side counterbalanced a minute or two later by one to the left, one to the shoulder complemented a few blows later by one to the wrist or hip on the other side. He saw she was going to cover his whole body with blows. Nothing less than that would satisfy her now.

After several minutes of this his entire body was stinging and burning, exquisitely sensitized, radiating specific layers of heat like a thermographic portrait. He began where he could feel precisely where the next blow would fall, could feel her circulating in the darkness, and the exact spot where she would emerge, could feel the spot where the blow would strike, cooling in anticipation, and the corresponding part of her body glowing as she began to make her move, as if she were in orbit, assembling in slow rotation around him.

An opposite succession of shapes, the curtained doorway, the wall of mirrors, the two walls of windows passed behind her, the slant of the partition, her feet gathering in the little threads of light that lined the floorboards, and as she stepped back dispensing them out again, in and back, the two of them closer and then back, as if trying to fit into a single outline, into a mutual stance.

There was a moment's awkwardness when they first went to touch, where they had to figure out how first to touch, and what they did was to grab elbows and give a shake, and she laughed, for which he was grateful, his prime fear at this point being of it proving all too ethereal. He'd lost his belt and she had shed her jacket somewhere along the way, and for the first time he noticed how flushed she was, her face and neck streaked with sweat.

They took turns holding each other's shoulder as they stepped out of their *gi*'s. Then they had to work out a position where neither of them would be dominant, that is to say, neither one of them subordinated, trying it first on their side, but they weren't able to work their legs out that way, then sitting up face to face—while he could feel the momentum siphoning off, the moment drifting off, and he turned her onto her back and quickly mounted her, fucking her and fucking her and fucking her until the point was effectively moot.

She exuded a faint workmanly odor, that he'd previously associated exclusively as a masculine odor, and there was a certain sense—a certain lack of rhythm in the frenzied parts, where she had the feel of a man. As she turned over on top of him, her arms braced behind his head, breasts pulled almost flat against her chest, her hips taut and almost flesh-less under his hands, he could almost imagine her a boy—but they were beyond that now, beyond differences now, it could as easily be her inside him now.

At one point he heard her speak and lifting his head thought he could hear her counting, *"Ich...nee..."* and felt the laughter welling up, but he suppressed that, pushed beyond that, out into a lengthening clarity where each isolatable shape in the room lay on a separate plane, each at an assigned distance with an absolute value from the next, fanning out in a backward progression counterclockwise around the room. Just as he was beginning to settle into that feeling, he felt himself start to draw over—pulled back, but a moment too late, so that he experienced the moment as a stumble and a loss. She urged him on, responding with a reserve of energy that he wouldn't have expected, that was hardly sexual—for she made no effort to pretend that this was her moment, too—drawing him closer, tighter, every part of her body that touched his body in motion, no motion at all required of him, drawing him down to a refinement of stillness where even pleasure seemed to lie in suspension.

At the peak, the very sweetest moment, she bent her head and lightly touched her lips to his eyelid, the corner of his mouth, the side of his nose.

Then for a long time they just lay, he on his back with her lying half on top of him, her head inside the crook of his neck. The skin across the top of his thigh was pinched up where she was sliding off him, and her wrist had gotten wedged up under his chin, but he focused on the discomfort of that as a way of fixing the moment, his head back, his eyes open, empty of any motive or idea.

Then gradually over the space of a minute or two, like in these speed-action films where the figure of Adam is formed out of bare dust, or a beautiful woman reverts to a wrinkled crone, the different sections of the room began to align themselves, and without either of them having moved, he could begin to distinguish her body from his own. Then she stirred, lifting up to readjust the position of her leg, and pushed back her hair. He'd gotten his ankle tangled up in one of the gi's. He tried to shake it loose, then bent down to free it, and when he lay back again, the two of them side by side now, he could feel them matching breaths, aware now of the rhythm and tone of her breathing.

Then they were both up—

"Did you see a—"

"Did you try over by the—"

His whole head and chest were radiating and tender like a sunburn. He'd wear this evening's entertainments for a few days to come. He wandered out into the hallway to look for a water fountain, and found a utility sink in one of the closets, letting his head and arms hang under the faucet, and then drip for a minute or two, and when he came back, she'd finished dressing and packing her *gi* into her bag. Seeing him standing there, she gave him a smile, an easy, contented smile, and it occurred to him, for the first time in a number of minutes, that for her all of this had been a combat, and that in her mind she'd probably won. He stood for a moment in the doorway trying to gauge the extent to which this was true, and to what extent it mattered to him.

"You see," she said as they were coming down the stairs, "it's just a matter of finding your own way of doing it."

He had just been thinking that if this was the only way he could do it, only proved the impracticality of doing it at all.

They came out the front way—there was a push bar on the front door that locked automatically behind you—and just as they were stepping out the door there was a rush and bustle from around the corner. Instinctively they took a step back and began to lower into stance, their shield arm raising— but it was only a couple of black kids, a boyfriend chasing his girlfriend, she pumping high-kneed and shrieking over her shoulder, he loping comically along behind, down the block and around the next corner. They looked at each other and laughed, a little embarrassed, and the easing up of that carried them the rest of the way down the block, but he could see an uncertain moment coming up here when they reached the cars and it came time to separate. But as they came around the corner—swinging wide, in case any vagrant should be lurking around the other side—he decided maybe not. Across the street, through a narrow gap in a low line of hedges, the van and car sat parked, in the nearest, lightest section of the lot, parked two or three spaces apart, so that even as they approached them their paths were diverging, and from here it was only a matter of a few more steps, a smile perhaps, a word or two, and then good-night.

EASY TO BELIEVE

There was one in the *Post-Gazette* she would like, a man on 51 hailed over by police for failing to stop for a red light, who decided to make a run for it, through the Tubes, across the Liberty Bridge and up the Boulevard of Allies, a fourteen-car chase finally at speeds over a hundred mph, until his engine blew out at the corner of Beacon and Wightman in Squirrel Hill.

This was a standard-wheel Pontiac, the man in his fifties and never had a traffic violation in his life before. His wife was riding with him at the time.

"I'd like to hear the conversation they were having while all this was going on," Wanda Proctor said.

McBride said, "I'd like to have heard the one they had that led up to it."

They were sitting around the table, going through the paper and waiting for Wanda's husband Max to get home so that they could all go out to eat. In his other ear Issabeth's sister Mary Pat was telling him some of the stories Wendy Soune had brought back from her last Russian trip.

"The Russians wanted to build a new resort in Bam, and it was going to be this huge national project and go up in a hundred days. Except there were no roads. There were no workers' quarters. It was disaster. So now there're all these rows of earth movers rusting out there in the wilderness. Though they did get a top-ten hit out of it, Bam Bam Bam," slipping down into bassetto, "City of One Hundred Days," and giving out a raucous snort.

"You know in Russian opera there's always all these tractors and road builders out on stage, and this one Russian opera where the World War Two pilot gets his legs shot off and in the end is rehabilitated, and they wheel a fighter bomber out on stage, and this one famous Russian faggot, critic, I forget what he is, has this thing for paraplegics, little boys, and on the opening night rented the first two rows of tickets—"

Wanda Proctor put up her arms and went, "Bork!"

145

Not the least McBride considered of the anomalies of his life in Pittsburgh was that he'd fallen in with the Russian contingent, a little settlement of expatriate poets that made not poetry so much as a series of poetical "stances," explicable mainly to themselves and the local FBI. Over in the living room section of the room, Wendy Soune, sitting very close on the couch to her new husband Misha, was telling some of her own Russian stories, about how after they were married and living in Vienna in the apartment of a Sasha who hadn't wanted Misha here to marry his first wife, and the KGB had followed them everywhere they'd go. Everybody in Wendy Soune's stories was named either Sasha or Misha, and was always being followed by the KGB everywhere they'd go. She and Mary Pat and Wanda's Max all worked for the same import-export firm downtown shipping pocket calculators into the Soviet Union, and it was only through the medium of Mary Pat, who expropriated them shamelessly, oftentimes right in front of her, that her stories achieved anything of their true Marxian savor. This Misha she'd met only on this last Russian trip, and married mainly as a way of helping out of the country, and now, literally before your eyes, was falling authentically in love with, the romantic coup of the season Issabeth called it.

"Have you told Issabeth any of these stories?"

"Where is our Izzybeth tonight? Anyway?"

"Doing the membership drive on QED. I'm picking her up at nine."

"Izzy's on TV? Why didn't you say so? So put her onnn."

McBride shook his head. "She doesn't want people watching. She says she'd rather people didn't even know she was being on."

"That means she's getting all dressed up. I'll bet she got all dressed up. Though. I'll bet she walks off with her own morning show."

McBride gave one of his little shrugs, which brought

another raucous snort out of Mary Pat, who'd been looking a little peaked this evening he'd been thinking. Issabeth had told him, and something Wanda Proctor had said earlier tended to confirm, that Mary Pat was doing a good deal of drinking lately, a quart of scotch a day Issabeth claimed, though you could discount a certain part of that, Issabeth seeming to feel you could perpetuate any sort of slander you wanted on your sister and have it turn out only the most outrageous sort of jest.

The problem was that they were so much alike, there was the eleven years' difference between them, and still they were that much alike. Mary Pat had the full shine, the full profusion of freckles, the coppery blaze of hair that in Issabeth was more muted now, a finer, subtler glow. She was a true beauty, in a way he imagined Issabeth had never been—she'd always had to place herself, hold a little back, where Mary Pat could be totally renegade and unchecked.

"—was saying these horribly indiscreet things," she was telling Wanda Proctor, "like how I slept on the bed and he was on the couch all night, and still he had a hard on the whole time, which proves how much he loves me. Still," like this habit she'd acquired lately of tagging words on after the end of her sentences, this growing reliance she was showing lately on mannerisms. Though at that age it could be a year or two, another three or four years, before the signs really started to toll.

Max Proctor came in then, conscious of keeping them waiting and covering for it by running a busy bustle all over the house, up the stairs and down to the basement, after a minute or two sticking his head through the kitchen doorway and saying, "Say, well, we probably ought to be going—"

He was the one McBride knew least, the one who seemed the most substantial to him out of the group—although a part of that, he'd been deciding lately, came maybe just as a function of not knowing him all that well. As they were going out the door, and McBride would have been the

147

last one out, he stopped and turned back inside for a moment, as if to attend to one final thing. McBride looked to see what it was, and it was nothing. He'd simply not been able to let anyone go out the door after him. He and Wanda wore these flat, understated colors, pale grays and drab earthen browns, always with a little swath of color, a scarf tucked in at the neck, or a thin strip of bright colored sleeve peeking from underneath the cuff of a sweater.

"Where's Izzy tonight?" he asked McBride as they were coming off the porch.

"Doing the pledge drive on QED. I'm picking her up after bit."

"Izzy on TV? You should have said something, we'd have put her on, oh—but she'd probably as soon people weren't watching."

It had been raining when he drove over, but had stopped now. At the bottom of the walk Mary Pat was telling Wanda Proctor one of her state cop stories, "—and I say, oo, but officer, you can't give me a ticket, my boyfriend's a state cop, you give me a ticket and he'll mur-dur me!" Everywhere she went Mary Pat created incidents, men following her on the street, taxi drivers pulling over to offer her rides—the latest of these always formed a reliable nucleus of any conversation with Mary Pat. For a long time he'd been convinced she was at least on some level the instigator in these—until one night about a month ago he'd seen her propositioned asleep on a barstool inside Three Brothers.

"—brother gets on the line and says, sure, Mary Pat, yeah, we know Mary Pat, what's she done *this* time?" eyes going wide, looking all around—"Oo, you're not all waiting for me, are you, I'm taking my car, I have to—" but that was lost on McBride.

He knew what that meant, though, that meant this would be the last they'd be seeing of Mary Pat this evening. Lately Mary Pat was always making separate arrangements for herself, and then losing herself in these separate arrangements.

As she was getting into her car, he walked over and wagged a big brotherly finger at her, saying, "You and I, young lady, are going to have to have a talk."

"Oo," making the eyes again, "we're going to have our talk, are we?"—with just the slightest underscoring, the smallest little pause in her voice.

Then as he turned to go back to his car, he saw the others still sitting in their car, and waved them on—"No, that's all right, I'm taking my car, too, I'm—" and there was a moment—a moment before there was a reaction, while they just stared out the windows at him.

Driving over, he brooded on it, it was a warning, a sign, there'd been several of these over the course of the evening. Here he was Mary Pat's sister's *impassionato*, a nebulous though a definite enough designation that any alteration in the level of interest he was able to inspire was enough to send alarm bells sounding all across his brain; stalled halfway down Negley Hill behind a line of cars backed up behind the pothole at the bottom of the hill, suspended like a ferris wheel car with the whole east-end view of the city spread out below him, shining and glittering after the rain like a carnival town, the eighth, tenth straight day of rain—he pushed all this to the front of his mind, as arbiter in any conclusions he might draw this evening: cold, gray thoughts on a gray, damp evening.

They met in the parking lot in back of Bouquet Street, really a three-block-long string of lots backing a three-block stretch of dance bars, leather shops and rock boutiques, a former movie house that was now the Theatre Mall, where Mary Pat, as anticipated, did not appear. They were also meeting the Sandmans, Mike and Patricia, here, and for a couple of minutes lingered by the cars, not so much expecting her as just deciding what restaurant to go to.

"Gone down."

"Too expensive. Nice but overpriced."

149

"And food's not that good."

"Oh, I know"—this from Wanda Proctor—"that place where Loaves and Fishes used to be Bards and Jesters, I was by there last Thursday and they were working inside, let's go see if that's open."

The entire surface of the pavement, not just where the light hit, shone creamy yellow, the sides of buildings, up the sides of the utility poles. He walked back with the Sandmans, who he didn't know well, taking this opportunity of drawing them out. They'd been in some kind of accident, Mike Sandman was walking with a cane, but it was old news and he wasn't able to sort out any details. They were so complimented he would show an interest in them. Mike kept telling about subsidiary screening, and watchdogging for opening opportunities, and of course you don't always want to be relying on your own initiative, until finally McBride said, "Well, what is it you do exactly, though?"

And he said, "Well, mainly is I talk to people who eventually want to get in to meet Patricia's dad."

What struck him was the ease, the perfect lack of any embarrassment with which this came out, more with a kind of modest understatement. Immediately all his interest in them faded. They were greeters—it was her, too—a certain style of ingratiating, a certain kind of children of the rich.

All the time they were walking, he was laying the street out in his mind, marking crossings, noting what windows had clocks in them. It was seven-forty now, even a little early still to be sitting down.

The building where Loaves and Fishes had been Bards and Jesters was down a short alleyway—mallway—with patterned brick paving and facsimile gaslamps, on either side a row of little shops, really two long rectangular buildings that had been broken into little shops. The new place, as yet unnamed, was next to the last on the left side, only a door and a window wide, both of them covered over with butcher paper. There was light showing through from inside, though, and high up on the left side of the window was a tear in the paper, through which you could look in, like into a diorama, at the ethnic family gathered around the table testing a tureen.

Wanda tried the door and knocked, leaned up to the tear and rapped and waved.

"Hey, can we come in? Hey?"

They were middle-eastern, McBride thought, until Max told him they were Peruvian, two married brothers, or two pair of cousins, or a pair of married sisters he finally decided, plus an old couple in back to take care of the cooking—like apparitions figures kept appearing out of the darkness bearing platters to be tasted. They insisted on their guests taking the chairs. There were nine tables and as yet only seven chairs. "Our first night of business we will give a free dinner to everyone who brings a chair. That way we will have our chairs." They were opening Friday, and as yet hadn't named the place, or settled on a menu. "You give us your name. We write down all the names, and then we will make our choice."

"But an American name," one of the men, the host-apparent of the group, told them. "All our food here will be American food. This is the vegetable soup."

The soup was glistening green, so bright green it was practically golden, and filled, he found when he blew onto a spoonful, with finely chopped carrot and bits of meat and maybe celery, and a tiny brown pea with a pale blue crescent along the seam.

"Also we have the chef salad and the hamburger sand-wich."

He did find out one thing while they were sitting there, how Mary Pat had come by her tan.

"She spent New Years in Fort Lauderdale with a dentist taking his qualifying exams," Wanda Proctor told him. "He'd already passed his writtens but had to take the practicals over, and they let you bring along your own cavity—"

McBride said, "I wonder if they throw the brushing in

151

for free?"

"Do you know what that means?" Wendy Soune asked her Misha—"high-speed brushing, dental brushes." She said a couple of words in Russian, and Misha smiled and made a little show of illumination. He was a nice looking, boyish-looking man, about twenty-seven or -eight, but with a kind of rubberiness of complexion that took age well, and missed being handsome only for having a nose that was too long. The Russians all had bad noses, McBride was thinking, Baryshnikov had a bad nose, Nureyev had a bad nose, too much partition showing, or too much on an angle with the rest of the face—and that was about his interest in the Russians. This one was a flautist, so they were branching out from mere poets into the other arts as well.

As if to echo this thought, Max said, "We're thinking about opening a branch in Istanbul this fall. Wanda and I may fly over there next month."

McBride said, "You're turning into a regular United Nations."

He was surprised at the reception this got.

"People just naturally assume," Wanda said, "the UN is ineffectual in everything it does."

"An institution," Max said, "an idea like the United Nations has a twenty-five, a thirty-five-year effectiveness factor it has to work inside. Its influence to date has been largely indetectable."

"Has to be," Wanda said, "if it's to have any influence at all. This new move is only the first of four we have planned for the coming year."

"Twelve months from now," Max said, "we'll be on four continents, and in fourteen different countries."

Life in the subjunctive mood. Over on the other side of the table Wendy Soune was describing how on this last Russian trip her luggage had been held up for four days, and when they finally gave it back they told her she just hadn't looked hard enough, and there was only this one little room, and everything had been turned inside out and all balled up, like they hadn't even tried to be subtle about it, though there had been nothing damaged or lost except for one of the crayons she had been bringing for Pasha's niece that was shorter than the others, as if they'd been using it to mark things or checking for microdots.

While beside him Mike and Patricia were going, "No, oh, they didn't!" and "How aw-ful!" and at the appearance of each new sample out of the kitchen, "Oh, isn't this grand? Oh, I'm so glad you invited us!"—professional enthusiasts, a pair of perpetual exclamation points, though it wasn't fawning, exactly, or even necessarily insincere. It was more a kind of mechanism they exercised. A few minutes after this, while he was standing beside them at the door, he heard them talking to each other, "Wasn't this nice? Yes, oh, aren't you glad they asked us!"

The old people he decided weren't to have that much to do with the operation after all, they gravitated toward one of the farther tables, that would be the family table, though the place was a little small he was thinking to be having a family table. That had been the problem the other two times, too small of a kitchen, not enough seatings to be supporting this many people.

But the place she would like, the place itself she would like. He'd bring her over here the night they were bringing the chairs, she'd enjoy that.

"Walk over to Spittin Image with us?" Wanda suggested.

"I have to pick Issabeth up first. Maybe we could meet you."

Still he had four or five minutes he could work around. McBride specialized in easy exits, the one element of social skill he still adhered to with any regularity. He was looser now, lighter, pointing them to a window display of giant kitchen implements, huge colanders and whips, drawing them in, drawing them along, creating little intimacies out of which his own departure would only seem a natural extension. Now he was tracing back the steps he'd laid out for himself earlier, checking the time in this and that window, matching discrepancies against the watch on Wanda's or Mike Sandman's wrist, planning out what route he'd take, picturing the moment she'd appear, the door opening, the moment just before he caught sight of her.

Driving over, he thought how much of his time was spent in this way, going to meet, waiting to meet a woman, how much these were the fullest, in many ways the most fulfilling moments that he spent, and yet how much too they were moments spent most intensely with himself, checking out and redefining, plotting small modifications in course, testing the nice feel of his topcoat across his shoulders, his name coming off his tongue—

"Bill McBride. Good evening, I'm Bill McBride."

He was still a little early the first time by, and drove up to the next light and turned around and came back, this time on the station side of the street. Almost as soon as he stopped, promptly enough that he knew she'd been watching, but with the requisite pause for effect, the doors swung open and she hurried out, in her black mink, hugging the collar to her throat and glancing back as if pursued. It was starting to drizzle again. The steps were standing slabs of the same slick brown granite as the sides of the building, and he leaned across the seat with one arm raised to caution her to watch her step.

She came down the steps stepping sideways and smiling into the car—while the little effervescence he'd been gathering up through the course of the evening slowly dissipated and was gone.

"You want to congratulate me, they say I raised nearly sixteen hundred dollars tonight, and I'm asked back again for Friday night, and Monday morning I go downtown to see about doing a Pittsburgh Is A Whole World Of People, have you eaten?"

"I had soup and rolls with Max and Wanda a bit ago, but

I could probably eat something more if you're ready. They want to know if we'll meet them at Spittin Image?"

"Oh—"

They came to Negley, where they would have had to turn off, and kept going, in the direction now of the house.

"Have you eaten?"

"They brought in sandwiches and fruit about seven. Actually I could probably wait, unless you're in a hurry. They had to take Sarah Giles out tonight, I don't know if you remember her, she's the one who had the husband who did his income tax year round. For a hobby. She answered a phone with the same hand she was holding a call-back slip, and the corner went in her eye, which was why he could never hold onto any girlfriend, Corleen would always have to sleep up on the bed with them. Though at $500 a litter I guess you could see where she would have certain prerogatives."

He'd missed a step or two here somewhere. She was leaning up to the windshield, wiping her cheeks with hard tissue strokes back from the nose.

"Her real name was Coeur de Lion, Heart of the Lion. We used to hide behind the door and listen to him talking to her while he did the dishes, What do you think about that, Coeur de Lion? What would you have said in a case like that, Coeur de Lion? We could always tell when he was freaked, he would pull whiskers out of his beard and stick them to the wall next to the toilet. What is it?"

He didn't say anything.

"Do you want to talk about it?"

"We could talk about it."

"Well, I don't knew whether we ought to talk about it. We talk about things I don't think are particularly important things, and by the time we're through talking about them, they've become very important things indeed. I'm thinking we'd be better off just talking around things."

"If you feel that way."

"If I feel that way."

They drove on a minute or two in silence. They were on Braddock now, had already passed the turnoff for the house. A little farther now and they could turn on Forbes and double back, or onto the Parkway downtown.

He said, "Or would you rather just drive a while?"

"It doesn't matter, we could just drive for a while."

She was sitting back now, piling her hair on top of her head and letting it fall. Underneath her coat her dress was iridescent green, the same yellow-green, oddly, as the soup he'd just eaten, the material drawn over the shoulders and held together by a big brass ring open at the cleavage, a dress that looked made for TV.

"He's the consummate jerkass, pe-pull. In Europe, pe-pull, you wouldn't own a TV, you'd pay a licensing fee to have a TV in your home. In Finland, pe-pull, you'd pay $79 a year—oh, and you know who else, this is from Rolf and Elsa days, Little Flower, from Flower and Hermes, she was so adorable, just angelic, they used to dance on the terrace in these flowing angel's robes. They've fixed her face up now, but it still isn't right, she looks as if she has to be at least thirty-five—"

She goes on, their names having come up, to recount the story of Rolf and Elsa's robbery last summer, a story he's heard before.

"I had the key and was to go in just to reset the alarm. There was a cassette recorder in the coats cupboard that on the slightest entry would telephone the police and their place in Ford City and one near neighbor, and they and the near neighbor were both being away for the month, and there was another neighbor who would hear the alarm and telephone me and I would go in after the police and everybody had gone and reset the alarm. There was a button you pushed and then had twenty seconds to get back out the door. Except that what they did was to take the panel out of the back door and roll up all the carpets and slide them out, except they didn't take quite all the carpets, they left the biggest and least nice one. These were the same discriminating bandits that were doing all the houses in upper Shadyside. They would go through a jewel box and take just the real pieces and throw the paste and glass all out on the floor—so you were getting not only your possessions stolen, but a critique on your taste as well."

Then to one he hadn't heard, about Elsa's New Year's Eve party.

"She's setting out the things and catches the cat in the salmon mousse, so she shoos kitty outdoors and smooths the damage over, but then later in the evening, when she goes out to the garage for more ice, she finds the cat dead on the garage floor. So she decides to take everybody down to the hospital to get their stomach pumped. And then the next morning her neighbor stops by and says he's found the cat run over in the street and put her in the garage and didn't say anything, because he knew she was having a party and didn't want to upset her evening."

He nods, answers, or doesn't, as the moment requires, not so much holding back or unwilling to respond as just wishing there could be a minute or two here where they could sort out and catch up, this constant backlog of things unsaid and left half said, he was convinced, the prime cause of their difficulty now. Other times she's reproached him for these silences. She finds them deliberate. "It's as if you make a policy of not relating to me."

They were downtown now, on their second pass by the old train station. "My father used to bring me down there when I was a little girl to watch the trains come in."

"Would you like to stop there now?"

"It doesn't matter. We could stop and look around."

There was a flat two-fifty parking fee, McBride trying to finesse and then kid his way by, finally tearing around and back through several blocks of traffic until he found a place on the street to park, marching triumphant back past the gateman, up the curving brick drive that led to the stone canopy that fronted the building. She had her letting-it-pass look on now. "Each archway bears the name of one terminus in the Penn Central Line, New York, Philadelphia, Pittsburgh, Chicago."

Through a set of swing doors—"No, over here"—through the ones with the electric eye, through a chilly vestibule and another set of swing doors, and out into a long, practically deserted waiting room, only two windows open, a black soldier repacking his bag next to a row of lockers, a man just passing through, a young woman seated on one of the farther benches—too scattered even to stand as representative figures. At an effort perhaps at modernization, one end of the floor had been dispansified with a section of false ceiling, a white acoustical slab hung down from a network of fine wires, an effect rather attractive in its own right. The rest of it was ornate and faded, chipped mosaic and yellowed cornices, not so much shabby as simply abandoned.

She shook out her collar, pushed back her hair, smiling a smile of aesthetic satisfaction.

"I have a friend, Norbert you know, owns the Klondike Internationale, who wants to buy this place and convert it to a discotheque. It would be ideal for crowds. There could be a bar," pointing to a long Passengers With Reservations Check Tickets Here counter, "and there, it's so sad, it's such a beautiful old place."

They read on a board where there would be a train in in another eighteen minutes.

"Did you know it was a dentist Mary Pat went to Florida with over New Years?"

"An endodontist, please. I told her he could as easily have taken her to California. They have the same kind of exam, and then they could spend their winters touring the sunbelt."

He caught a hint here, the same small lag of response he'd noticed earlier from Mary Pat and the others in the car, she thought he was making a play for Mary Pat, that's what all of them thought, a complication on top of so many other complications too complicated even to begin to think of sorting out.

He wandered over to a side alcove where there were cracker machines and pinball machines, dropped a quarter into one of the pinball machines, and let it play, fingers to the flippers, feet poised, but making no effort to affect in any way the destiny of the ball, and when that ball dropped pulling the lever and letting another one play, and another one on through until the last one had dropped, having registered what he imagined to be the minimum count.

He found her at the doors marked Trains. She took a step, and with a mighty whoosh the doors sprang open. She grinned over her shoulder at him, and took a step back, and with a sorrowing sigh they drifted closed again.

They passed through another deserted vestibule, where a row of ring radiators hissed ineffectually underneath perforated yellow canisters, through another set of swing doors, and out onto the platform.

Overhead a high girdered roof offered a nice ambiguity between indoors and outdoors. All down the track big knuckle valves were shooting out clouds of steam, "like in every train movie you ever saw," each one attached at the handle to a long, convoluted plume of milky ice, odd "because you know it's really not that cold out." They passed a man in a glass room backed by a wall of instruments, and a man walking the other way. But other than them, the place was completely deserted.

A little way down the tracks a train was parked. "I want one I can run alongside and wave a hankie to." It turned out to be a farther walk than it appeared, and when they got there it was deserted, the cab windows blanked out, "a ghost train." The cars were almost all flatcars, each one loaded with a separate trailer rig.

"You know most of the traffic nowadays is carrying trucks cross country. It's cheaper than loading up and unloading and paying gasoline."

She was half turned, her head backlighted against a giant bulb on top of a pole on the other side of the tracks. There was a fine furriness, usually obscured by freckles, and almost transparent in the light, across her cheeks, and he reached, almost reached toward her, but held back, a necessary caution having entered into their reactions now, with so many mistimed and misspent gestures, each, by some berserk law of proportions, adding up to attritions four, sixteen, sixty-four times outside all expectation.

Just then she turned and slipped easily into his arms, pressing hard, her whole body against his, and then, in a style they'd fallen into lately, going lax, her head tilted back and drooping to the side, exposing a glistening trough of skin between the two long bones of her neck where he might plant his lips.

The train pulled in and ten or twelve men in khaki got off, each carrying a lunchpail, and went on inside.

"You notice how most of the people that ride the trains these days are people that work for the railroads. If we were in Europe right now, this place would be jammed with people."

Back past the man in the glass room, through the vestibule of the hissing radiators and back across the waiting room and through the outer lobby, a little dip and a smile each time they passed through one of the swinging doors, "You'll notice how they work only when you're coming in, not as you're going back out again," he saw it would all go like this now, there would be no acrimony, no scenes, she would never be anything less than kind.

They came out onto a brick mandela floor—the mirror of the lining of the canopy overhead—where a lone taxicab sat parked, its driver asleep across the wheel. The dome of the canopy rested on four minor canopies, supported on short pilasters disguised as clusters of slender columns. She walked underneath the arches, he on the outside along the railing, one, and then another of the pilasters passing between them, and then a slow diagonal walk across the floor of the canopy, neither of them looking at each other, past the dry stub of a fountain, her face pointed straight ahead in a kind of example of composure, and as the next of the pilasters cut between them he had the notion that when he looked again, she would be gone, have disappeared, and he looked and she was still there, and as the next, the last one before the drop down to the street cut between them, he stopped, not breaking down and not faltering exactly, but just unready for those few seconds to take that next step—although he did think afterward that he might have manufactured the moment, as a way of making her come to him, which after a minute she did, her head coming around the side of the pillar questioning and a little fearful, "Bill?" reaching tentatively to touch his arm, "Sweetheart, is something the matter? What is it? Isn't it something we can talk about?"

THE LID

"Where'd you say this comes from?" Tahlar asked, as Adrian was loading up the second pipe.

Tahlar was a pacer. Two or three tokes, and it was up and down the rug. Adrian, on the other hand, sat solid, only the eyeballs moving now, omnivoyantly, an effect Tahlar found distracting and contrived.

"This is Ecuadorian. This one is thirty-five a lid. Also I have another one I can let you try that's twenty a lid, or two for thirty-five. This one grows above the tree line. The peons carry water up in clay jars to feed it. Can I offer you anything, by the way? Pepsi? I have Sprite, Millers, iced tea?"

At the same time, without getting up, without really turning, he was changing the record on the machine.

"That one you just heard was chimes from the Belgium World's Fair. This one now is Hearsall, Anton Corle. Every fifth fiche reverses itself and plays backwards for a bar, what would be the equivalent of a bar. They're mirror movements, what Corle calls paired utterances."

"Vector recurrences," Tahlar read from the back of the album cover. "No, just water's fine for me, thanks."

He considered for a moment. He'd followed through the different offers of refreshment, and halfway down the first column of liner notes, and through a cost-quality analysis of the different stained-glass outlets in the area, but lost it now in what was either the plot for some science fiction novel, or the account of an especially taxing evening.

"Where'd you say this came from?"

"This one is Ecuadorian. This one I can let you have for thirty-five, or I have another one you can try that's twenty, or two for thirty-five. This one is a very subtle dope. After a while you forget you're stoned, until maybe half an hour, three-quarters of an hour later, you feel it start creeping up on you all over again."

"I'll—tell—you—what—take one of these now maybe later's a friend been asking me to be on the lookout, I can get back to you."

More promptly, with a good deal greater agility than Tahlar would have expected, Adrian was on his feet, the ounce was proffered, money exchanged, a small pharmaceuticals bag provided for carrying the purchase—his skeleton seeming to assemble itself bone by bone underneath the skin as he moved around, until now he hulked over Tahlar, looming and inobstreperous, all expression blanked out by the sheer mass of him.

Tahlar appreciated the ease, the efficiency by which the operation, once completed, delivered him at the door. He detected a little coolness maybe on the way out, Adrian having read into his reluctance to commit himself to a second ounce some aspersion of the product, but if so that was all right, one of his main reservations about Adrian up until now being that he'd found him a bit too stolid, a visceral reaction he was thinking now against fat people, although that was another thing, too, that you were careful while you were discounting that you weren't also plowing acres of significance into every little chest heave and eyebrow bounce.

He was interesting, though, with his library records, and his synopses, and his pop bottles. It turned out he worked at a reclamation center, and this time had brought a couple cases of his collection out to show Tahlar, Red Scotty Sodas with the shingled neck and the leaping scottie dog on every bottle, Canice Brs. Bottlers, R. Stimmell Beverages. Every man his own bottleer. Of course he had his games, like always offering the sample in a water jar, which Tahlar felt tended to enhance a mediocre weed, and his Tahlar suspected intentionally disconnected spiel, although a lot of that you had to accept for standard dealer rep.

He had a half-faded stamp on the back of his hand, what on his previous visit Tahlar had assumed to be a stamp, but realized now was a tattoo, of the letters GLOVE.

Then at the top of Forbes it was Friday, it was Halloween Friday and he had two invitations to go to that evening, and as he came out from under the overpass at Allies into the sunlight he passed the Snakes van, a big silver van with a huge striking cobra on the side, and the blue Connecticut plates SNAKES, and at the crest of the hill where the cones had been knocked over and the line tracked back and forth like possibilities crossing and recrossing, he was thinking Adrian Lore was turning out not to have been such a bad find after all.

After dinner, while he was cleaning the ounce, the phone rang with a third invitation, Jennifer from Bixby's, from Jennifer and Lee, from the Thomasylum from three years back.

"I wouldn't be able to make it before late," he told her. "Really, I don't always lead such a popular life."

"Come whenever," Jennifer said, "it'll be just some people sitting around the floor."

By now he'd arrived at a firmer estimate, and was rolling in the special plum papers he reserved for his choicer blends. Five of these he stuck behind the toad bank on the mantelpiece, took five more upstairs for the letter basket on the shelf above the bed, and then split the remainder into two baggies, one for the triangle box on the left speaker, the other one for carrying, out of which he rolled five more for his pocket.

He was wearing his hollyhock shirt and J-tooled boots, and as he was on his way out the door, came back inside and put on his Cheyenne jacket, which he hadn't worn since it'd come back from the cleaners. Most of the beads were broken off the fringe now, and there were dark spots at the elbows and down the back which the cleaning had only enhanced, but he liked that effect, the seasoned effect, and for a couple of minutes stood at the bathroom mirror, smoking another joint and admiring it on him.

He stopped off at the Big House first, first because that would be the easiest one to get away from. This was to be the last of the Big House parties, the place was going condominium in December. The Big House was an old brick mansion on Roselawn that had gone through several generations now of a law students' cooperative, with a swimming pool in back, and an oak-lined billiards room, and tin ceilings on all the upstairs rooms. They had two parties a year here, on Fourth of July and Halloween, and for this last one Tahlar estimated there had to be close to four hundred people, all of them wearing a resolutely bright and affirmative expression, as if they suspected this was going to be the last for them, too.

He sat on the front stairs with Lee Fairless, watching the different contingencies file by on their way to one or another of the upstairs rooms for their smoke.

"Conglomerations," Lee Fairless was saying, "something that could happen only once and then never happen again. People who have been through that much and go back that far together."

He watched the geometrics of the party form, introductories and preliminary resumes around the beer keg, exploratories and consolidations in the archways, intricate color migrations, red, brown, and then a long line of yellow working through the crowd.

"—so the one kid's dead and we're dealing with that," Lee Fairless was telling him, "and then we get a letter from his attorney saying they're only turning over two of the kids, the other one's in this mental reclamation program and can't be moved. Five years old and she's in a reclamation program?"

Tahlar fell in with a contingency of his own, up to one of the third-floor rooms, where thirty-five joints had to make do for nine people, and then wandered around for a while downstairs, dropping impressions.

Sets were big again this year, a princess and a pea, a

brace of jolly beefeaters, a flock of paunchy bees with a stern beekeeper who kept following them around with a big stick saying, "Now, you be-have!" Posted at the archway into the plant room was a pair of hula sisters, smiling complacently.

"Where's your costume?" they asked him.

"I'm the Duc de Rigueur," he told them. "It's a very subtle costume, you night not even notice it for a costume."

They crinkled their noses up at that.

In the spirit of the evening, everybody wanted you to know exactly who they were.

"No, not an efficiency expert quite," a young lady in a black cat's costume told him. "What I do is I write training programs, though what I have to do is study and reorganize the job so I can design the training program for the job I've already streamlined, so in effect you could say I'm an efficiency expert."

Five paces beyond her he met a white cat who had a theory of sevens, you were one of seven other, six other persons, men, though it might as easily be women as well, who led variations of extensions of lives complimentary with a ple as well as a pli to your own.

Standing next to her was a man dressed as what turned out to be a sprig of catnip, who was collecting slide rules. "It's only been fairly recently we've stopped manufacturing slide rules. People forget it's only been the past five or six years we've begun making pocket calculators."

He was overheard by a man on Tahlar's left who would like to get hold of a few HP35's, the original Hewlett-Packard calculators that had sold initially for four hundred dollars and now were selling for twenty-five, that had an error figuring the logarithm of 2.002 back exponentially to 2.000 instead of to 2.002, "like a misprint on a postage stamp."

Five or six years ago, as recently even as a year or two ago, he would have taken such congruities as evidence of a higher order in his life, but now he only saw them as evidence that the banality of the present age was finally reaching cosmic proportions. After a while he was only listening to the buzz words, quote unquote, heuristics and maneuveristics, effectivists and compounders, the ancillary hermeneutic and the textual ensemble, satisfice, as in when you come to a point where you know you can't succeed with what you set out to do, and you do a satisfice.

However he did run into his wife, who he only met anymore at these occasions, and watched a three-legged man do a three-legged merengue so convincingly you couldn't tell the fake from the real legs, and when he left there, around 9:45, after a brief aside into the nitrous den, it was with the high rising tide of the evening riding fast in his brain.

He had some difficulty finding Hope's, looking on Stanley rather than Standish. Outside of Hope's he met Ned Askin with a girl he'd met before, one of the women that owned Pwetty Kitty.

"How's the party?" he asked them. The front door and the curtains were all open, but the storm door and windows were steamed up, and the only people he could see inside were standing with heads bowed, as if in benediction.

"Casino concept," Ned Askin told him. "They give you two thousand dollars in play money when you come in to buy drinks and gamble with. Actually it's not so bad as it sounds. We're going over to Jeanne's brother's now to see about a water heater, but then we may be back."

"Hel-lo, Tahlar."

"Hel-lo, Jeanne."

Ned pulled a fat joint out of his shirt pocket, "Try some weefer, mon?"

"Ha-ho, amigo," whipping out one of his own, "weef some of thees."

They faded back into the shrubbery and toked up, after each hit turning the tips around to sniff the bouquet.

"Nice."

"Nice."

A troop of nascent Darth Vaders filed by, followed by a

miniature of the Watergate conspiracy, the Haldeman of which pointed the finger at them and went, "Naal! We smell what you're doing!"

On the top floor of an apartment building across the street, on the top floors of two adjacent apartment buildings across the street two bad bands were playing. From somewhere down the block came an uproar of dogs.

"One more into the dog pit," Ned said.

"We had my great-grandfather's ninety-second birthday today," Jeanne said. "We kept saying, 'You're ninety-two today, grappa,' and he'd say, 'We're a good group' and 'That's right, you go ahead and do what you want to.' He conceives of his purpose now as endorsing whatever people around him are doing."

"Nice."

"Nice."

"I think you're gonna like this party," Ned said. "Myself, I don't usually care for concepts, but these people are cool, they give you some space, they don't push it too far."

Thirty seconds inside the door, Tahlar remembered it had been Ned Askin's idea of a joke, when they were both interning at PUC, to slip bogus call-back messages into people's mail drawers. Situated around the room were tables for Risk, backgammon, Monopoly, at the last of which a hot procedural dispute was currently in process. The dining room table was set with a miniature roulette wheel, the doorway into the kitchen blocked by a combination bar and currency exchange, the mirrors outlined with tiny flashing Christmas tree lights. On all the doorframes neatly lettered signs pointed downstairs to pool and pinball, upstairs to chess and checkers and little boys and little girls, too charming, too outright earnest really even to be laughable.

But then he was too casual about turning back some of the money he'd just been handed to pay for his drink, and his hostess, who the last time he'd seen her for chrissake had given him head in the stairwell of Scaife Hall after a Civil

Procedures final, scowled sternly at him, and as he was turning away his head banged the dining room fixture, a stalactitic assembly of eighty sharply pointed brass prongs suspended from a pyramid of eighty tiny milk-glass globes, several of which were knocked atilt by the impact. He paused just long enough to arrest the swing before clamping his hands to his aching head—and a couple of the young men who'd been standing around the roulette wheel reached carefully up to right them, while a couple of others on the other side of the table pointed to others that still needed attending to, the sympathies of the group clearly with the fixture rather than his own aching head. And every time his fringe swayed, he could feel little scatter-shots of disapproval coming back over shoulders at him.

The only ones he knew here were the Cassadys, Bo and Becky Cassady, sitting on the couch in the front room, whose year at Child Advocates had been starting just as his own was finishing up.

"Oh, *no*," Becky told him, "we're from Queens, both of us. We grew up four blocks from each other. Though we were engaged four years before we got married."

She wiggled and worked her eyes, clasped her hands to her throat as if to strangle herself.

"Four years?" her husband broke in incredulously, "more like five years and eight months."

His tone said something special and private, probably lascivious, should be read in here.

"We were separated a year and eight months while Bo was at Cambridge," Becky said.

"No, and we weren't constant to each other all that time, either," Bo said, "we tried other people, both of us"—and they laughed uproariously, both of them.

Tahlar regarded them glumly. For a long time he'd been looking at this time in Pittsburgh as a term in exile, a little settlement of three or four or however many years it took him, free from the competitiveness and chicanery of the big centers, from what was after all only a provincialism of its own order, where he could assemble his style, polish up whatever little train of vehicles was going to take him streaming out of this happy burgh. But lately, just this past year, he'd been finding things in people that two or three years ago would have seemed to him perfectly negligible, like these two here, who two summers ago he'd sat the better part of an entire evening with on Tim Mears' back stoop, or Hope in her whimsy, Hope in her whimsy, he was sorry to see, like so much else around them lately having taken an institutional turn, seemed to him now the *ne minus ultra* of oppressiveness, a decline, maybe not a decline so much as a dislocation of values, some virus of proportions, the fallout probably of some huger contamination now working its way around the atmosphere—wondering if it was the dope he had to thank, the accruing experience of the dope breeding out in him a detachment, in which such dim verdicts more and more were the only ones available. Or if it wasn't just the quality of his associations.

He tried out the man on the right of him, who turned out to be doing work in the acquaintanceship pool—"We've determined every person has an acquaintanceship pool of 300 to 2000 people, persons you could identify by name, might recognize on the street. We estimate you can give any person a city directory and point out a name at random, and within five to seven person moves they'll be able to make personal contact—" then wandered downstairs to check out the pool match, after a minute or two by the way suggesting a joint to one of the young men who were standing against the wall, who as tactfully declined it, and a couple minutes after that he left, saying good-night to nobody.

"I have to keep track of the time," were his first words inside of Jennifer's, "I have some people coming over at 11:30 to watch *Wings of Man*."

There were six of them in a close circle on the rug, and all conversation halted the minute he walked through the door. He pegged the place at two-fifty, two-seventy-five, beamed ceiling, ripple plaster walls, some nice pieces but barren looking. They hadn't entirely moved in yet, Jennifer told him, a joke, they'd been here almost six months now, Joel, Bobby, Martinique, her roommate Gail, Jim and Joanna.

Jim was the clown of the group, a doggy-eyed, no-big-difference-to-me kind of clown, a manner he might have worn more comfortably two or three years ago than he did here tonight. He strummed lazily on a guitar, every now and then looking up and around with a lolling, sidelong grin that invariably brought surprised bursts of laughter from the others in the group.

He gave Jennifer a look and said, "Well, the world's biggest shovel broke down this afternoon."

"It didn't!" she exclaimed happily.

"They got it up there and now it won't start and the union won't lay a hand on it."

"Where's this?" Tahlar wanted to know.

"Ah," a trifle downcast, "Reddy."

He worked, as closely as Tahlar could tell, as a quality control inspector (though not a quality control inspector quite) at Reddy on Neville Island—his reluctance to supply this information speaking to his fear. Unrolling the baggie, licking a pair of papers together, Tahlar surveyed them again. They were all quality control inspectors, sales representatives, sold space for the symphony program, they were their promise made flesh, they were approachable only on the level of their fear. They were all watching to see how Jim would be accepted by him, as a gauge of how all of them would accept him.

He picked a few flakes off the carpet and deposited them back into the baggie, which prompted somebody to say it must be pretty good stuff. He'd smoked two at home before going out, rolled four more upstairs at the Big House out

of the bag, plus one outside of Hope's with Jeanne and Ned—
which ought to have left two more still in his pocket.

"Where's this from?" Jennifer asked as the second joint
was starting around.

"This is Ethiopian. This is a very subtle dope. After a
while you forget you're stoned, and then it comes back to
you—like maybe around the middle of Monday morning
you'll feel yourself starting to get stoned all over again."

There was a moment before they realized he was kidding, and the pause gave impetus to the laugh. He rolled two
more and set them out on the carpet in front of him.

"Jim has a theory," said Jennifer, "there are only two
hundred people really in the world."

"Oh, how's that?" Tahlar wanted to know.

"It comes out," Jim pondering, a bit plodding, "when
you're sitting in the bus terminal in DeKalb and the girl the
two guys on the next bench are talking about turns out to be
Joyce Sobine."

They all had a laugh on that, Tahlar most enthusiastic-
ally of all.

"You liked that?" Jennifer said.

Tahlar worked his head, too overcome to come back.

Gail said, "We're having dinner at Joanna's and there's
all this debris left on the table, shrimp skins and olive pits,
and lemon from the iced tea, and Joanna and I wrote this
song, it's called the 'Big Dinner Blues'."

She and Jim came in together, "Oh the pain, Oh I'm
sore, I'll never eat that much no more," Jennifer reaching
behind the couch for a banjo and joining them on the refrain,
"Cause I get them Big Dinner Blues."

> *Get the Alka Seltzer fast*
> *Don't know how much longer I can last*
> *When I got them Big Dinner Blues.*

Clear the johns
Clear the hall
I can hear ol' Mother Nature call
*Now I got them Big Dinner Blues.**

Bobby came in at the end with a harmonica wail, and for a minute or two after that the balance was so palpable that nobody wanted to risk it with a word.

"This is all right dope," Jennifer said finally.

"This is my special occasion dope," Tahlar said. "I keep it for my special occasions."

Somebody said, "Oh, is this a special occasion?"

"Except you know, anytime I smoke it turns out to be a special occasion."

They liked that, and it reminded Gail of the man in the desert who meets the Jew with the water flask, the Italian with a chair, and the Polack with the car door.

"When I tell it," Jennifer said, "I always let him meet them one at a time."

Smoothly with the line, "So I can roll the window down if it gets hot," Jim was in with his guitar, Jennifer reaching back to get her banjo, their voices blending on the first words of a new song.

The allocation of conversation to song was so carefully apportioned, the pace of the evening so finely tuned, and his own slim social gift, a gift for quick enthusiasm and easy laughter, carried him so effortlessly along, that when 11:15 came he was almost tempted to stay on—his hestitation causing him to announce too abrupt a departure, and there was an awkward minute here, while he was half risen on one arm, leaning in to hear the rest of what Martinique had started to say about alternate futures—"except the thing you start to find out about these alternate futures is that once you settle on one, you're locked into it"—and he could feel the circle closing in behind him.

Before he could leave, Jennifer took him around to

show him the rest of the apartment. It was the size of the rooms, the length of the hallway that she appreciated about the place.

"It's like when you ask anybody how they are, and they say I'm getting by, or I'm half making it, people never ask themselves anymore whether they're happy or not, just how well they're coping."

She opened two big walk-in closets to show him, and the door to the bathroom to show him the big claw-foot tub, her fingers lingering over the doorframes, the joy of possesion lighting up her face, and as she turned, just in the way her finger pressed the point of her chin, there was a reminder of prior days—just a word or two, the right gesture now would be all it would take to channel it.

"How've you been, Tahlar?"

"Oh, I had a little case of the skids around February, but I'm sixty-five thirty-five now."

She smiled at that, as if adding up to herself all his better qualities, and there was a special emphasis in her goodnight, but as he stepped back, even as the door was closing, she was already turning, her lips forming the first words of another song.

He was sitting on the couch, one shoe off, listening to Lunchbox chew her way around the new bag in the garbage pail. She knew better than to meddle in the garbage itself, but everytime he put in a new bag would chew the whole way round the inch or two he turned over the rim of the can. He wasn't especially aware of waiting for a call, but as soon as the phone rang knew that for the past fifteen minutes he'd been doing nothing else.

"How're you this evening?"

"Marlene. Hello."

She called every three or four weeks, always on a Friday evening, always just before midnight. More and more these

past couple of months, without actually admitting to himself
that he was doing it, he'd been arranging to be here by that
time.

"And what're you up to these days?"

"Not much, not too much, in fact. In fact, I just got in.
I was just sitting here taking off my shoes."

She would never so much as say she wanted to come
over.

"But I could always put them back on again."

"No, that's okay, I have my car. I forgot the address, is
all."

She parked a little way down the street, a blue Camaro
with Ohio plates, he knew from seeing out the window one
of the other times that they were Ohio plates. He'd met her
in Chances-R, the place with the two fronts, in February, a
couple of weeks before it burned down, and then for a long
stretch over the summer hadn't heard from her, and then ran
into her again in Three Brothers over Labor Day weekend.
He'd forgotten her name from the first time, and was never
sure afterward if it was the same as she'd given him before.
And he was never positive that she remembered his own
name. In the pattern they'd adopted, nothing was offered,
nothing asked, this air of assiduous mystery she so carefully
maintained, part, he suspected, of some private triumphal
march—to which he was the only too willing accomplice.

"Place looks the same."

She was wearing a fleecy black coat with a black fur
collar, a sequined dress so deep red it was virtually black,
black enamel bracelets the size of manacles crowding her
wrists, against which the scarlet maroon of her lips and her
fingernails was striking, she was in every way striking. She
was only nineteen, though for a long time he'd imagined she
must be considerably older.

"I was dating college boys when I was fourteen and fifteen," she told him, "I've always looked at least twenty-one."

She sat on the hassock, he behind her on the arm of the

chair, rubbing the back of her neck with his knuckle and the ball of his thumb until she tilted her head back and rolled it side to side. Then he said, "Want to go upstairs?"

She thought it over a moment and then said, "All right."

Each time the same, the moment of hesitation before answering, the head back, the hassock, but it was the ease and economy of the movement that tantalized him, that kept it from going stale.

Hands behind her back, dress suddenly dropping— "Whoopsie!"—her mouth going into a big O.

That cracked him up, that was charming. They sprawled across the bed, nuzzling and laughing.

He reached into the letter basket above the bed, "Something here I'd like you to try. Friend gave it to me. I've been saving it till you came by."

She puffed experimentally, big pucker-bite puffs, after each one holding the joint out at arm's length.

"It's something I keep here for special occasions," he told her. "Except, you know, every time I try one of these, turns out to be a special occasion."

She liked that. She said, "I told you about the man who's been paying me two hundred dollars a week to look at restaurants with him."

She hadn't, but he nodded anyway. He took off the rest of his clothes and got under the covers.

Three weeks ago a man walked up to her in Story's and offered her two hundred dollars to quit her job and help him open up a restaurant. He handed her two clean hundred-dollar bills, and it had taken him three weeks now to work around to an actual proposition.

"Today we're having lunch with the liquor supplier. I know a little bit about that, more than he does, anyway. Then we stop off to look at a restaurant—this is not our restaurant. The idea, see, is we're planning for this restaurant. Then we stop off for drinks. This is three in the afternoon. This is the work day. And he says to me, I have a restaurant in Fort Lauderdale I'd like you to take a look at."

"He says—"

"A restaurant in Fort Lauderdale that he'd like me to look at."

She was kneeling on the bed facing him, in black lace panties and bra, a thin red ribbon worked around the borders, her breasts pushed out over the tops of her bra, her hands making excited little pattycakes as she talked. The only light was what came up from the stairwell, reflected in silver arcs across her cheek and jawline and down the curve of her arm, like smaller bowls stacked inside of larger.

"So we go ahead and make the plane reservations, discuss whether we're going to have time for dinner here or should we wait till we get down there, all very businesslike. Meanwhile, he's telling me about this restaurant in Toledo he'd also like me to have a look at, and he says why don't we just stay overnight at his place in Palm Springs."

She tells him she needs to go home and pick up some things, but he tells her not to bother, he'll get her whatever she needs once they're down there. So then she asks about the sleeping arrangements, of course there'll be separate sleeping arrangements, and he says no, they'll be sleeping together, and she says oh no, they won't.

"And then he gets really mad at me and says, 'You're not old enough to be making these kinds of decisions.' "

"Says—"

" 'You're not old enough to be making these kinds of decisions'."

So he takes her home, she convinces him she has to get her own things, and she's to wait there until he calls her, and she has her mother write out for her what she's to tell him, "I want to keep working for you, but don't feel secure enough in the relationship just now to go out of town with you."

She's already mentioned by way of Toledo that her father lives in Cincinnati, so it's her mother in Pittsburgh and her father in Cincinnati, which was why the Ohio plates. And why for the long stretch over the summer he didn't hear from her.

He lay with his head against the wall, the roach pinched between two fingers, more paper now than roach, and more ash than paper, watching her through sleepy eyes. "Wonna" she said for wouldn't have, I wonna wanna, but he liked that, that tickled him, if he was afraid of anything with her now it was of it being all too much smooth turns and easy chances. In a minute now there'd be some discrepancy, a piece of information too many, a dropping of scales, a turn for the worse, that sad familiar retreat back from or weary advance on into the ordinary.

But for now she held, with her wonna, in the way she didn't completely undress just yet, in the way she hunched over him as she laughed. "So he calls me, it's ten-thirty now and I've gone over to my friend's to have dinner and left the number where he could reach me—" her lips a silvery gloss, that in a minute she would plant on his lips. In a minute she'd touch his knee through the sheet, or he would touch her arm just below the elbow, and she'd spread in a single motion like casting out into water her whole body on top of him, and if that wasn't satisfusion, he'd like to know what was.

* Lyrics for "Big Dinner Blues" courtesy of Janine Tulenko and Sandra Preuhs.

THE SUNDECK

It was only the second place he looked at, a *ct ocvw cvn bch shppng* the flier called it, cute he knew by now meaning small, and an oceanview a matter largely of rendition, on Chancery Lane several long loops up from the beach. The first floor was all garage, the upper floor just the two apartments, this one and the larger one next door, the bar and shaft of an L, with the sundeck running between.

Inside wasn't more than an efficiency, a narrow living room-bedroom, a kitchen, a small bath. But the walls were pine-panelled, and there were dimmer switches on all the lights, and from the corner windows the same good view of the water, and it took Peter Mikovich less than two minutes after walking through the door to agree to take it.

He was twenty-nine, a contract lawyer, newly divorced and newly transplanted from the East, and this for him was the epitome of California living.

Every evening at sunset time his neighbors, the Holsters, took Bloody Marys down to the end of the deck, underneath the hummingbird feeder, and had their time together. The hummingbirds came just at sunset, flitting two and three at a time after the emburnished liquor that trickled down the spiralling tube.

The Holsters were a handsome couple, tall, athletic, deeply tanned. Dr. Holster, or Dr. Joe as he'd rather be called, was a dentist, a quick, affable man in his early sixties, always ready to agree with whatever anybody said to him. His wife was a somewhat younger woman, a woman of around forty, blonde, smiling, and with a look, a typically California look Peter thought, of sleepy inconsequence. Her name was Beverly.

"Mr. Mikovich"—this on the day he'd painted his name on the mailbox below—"care to have a drink with us?"

"Say, all right, but call me Peter why don't you, or Mickey, most everyone calls me Mickey."

"Mickey."

"Mickey then it is."

They stood at the deck divider, discussing the composition of the liquid that went into the hummingbird feeder, the possible name of the climber that wound along the railing.

"These jitneys"—the merits of jitneys were much in the news around this time. The town was something of an artists' colony, and recently a fleet of bright colored jitneys, with striped awnings and wheel covers, had gone into operation on the streets. "You know, I think these jitneys ought to be allowed."

"My feelings," Dr. Joe agreed, "my feelings exactly."

"They're slow, it's true, and they tie up traffic, but they add color to the town. Color I think's important in a town like this."

"Exactly," Dr. Joe agreed, "my feelings exactly."

Besides the two of them, there was also an aged grandmother, who they sometimes pushed around the deck in a wheelchair, and a girl of high-school age named Lana, or Lannie, a slimmer, blonder, somewhat morose replica of her mother. Lannie wore an elaborate bracework across her teeth, which made her excruciatingly self-conscious. When Peter came in from work in the afternoons and she was out on the deck studying, she would hold her book up in front of her face until he'd gone inside.

He saw her in the evenings sometimes, too, practicing her dancing in the living room, turning round and around the room with slow, introspective steps.

One night after he'd lived there about a month, he came in to find a note pinned on his door.

"Mickey—dinner Friday night? Say 7:15?"

He responded in kind, with a note on their door, "Glad to!"

Promptly at seven-fifteen that Friday he came out his door and went into the pantomime of the man going out for the evening. They greeted him with applause. They'd carried the dining room table out onto the deck, and dressed it up with a lace tablecloth and brass candelabra and a big bowl of fruit for a centerpiece. Peter had brought along a bottle of wine, which they opened with great ceremony, pouring a little out into each of the glasses.

A sunset glow lay across the rooftops, the rims of the glasses, the floorboards of the deck.

"To the present moment," Dr. Joe proposed.

Dr. Joe, dressed in comic chef's apron and chef's cap, spread five thick meat patties onto the grill and sprinkled them with seasoning.

"You won't find a better burger than here, my friend," he said to Peter. "This is pure filet mignon, pure top inspected beef."

"It's pure extravagance," Beverly said.

"It's extravagant," Dr. Joe agreed, "but it's worth it. It's worth it to watch the butcher's face when I tell him grind it."

Beverly was dressed all in white, a trailing white dress that bared her shoulders and the greater part of her back, a fringed white shawl that she drew close around her, and then with a little shrug and a sigh, let drop down around her elbows, white lipstick and eyeliner, white nail polish. She lighted the candles on the table, went inside and put Chopin on the deck speakers, and came back out again carrying an assortment of miniature Chihuahua bells, which she spread out across the tabletop for Peter to inspect, picking up each one in turn and giving it a tiny tap of a satiny fingertip.

Gradually as the evening wore on Peter began to see it was she really who ruled the family. It was she who instructed Dr. Joe when to turn the meat, and Lannie in the laying out of the table. The old grandmama sat down at the end of the table in her wheelchair, wrapped up in an afghan.

Beverly hovered over her, arranging her plate.

"We're having corn, Mama, you like corn, I'll trim it off the cob for you and salt and butter it. This is fresh farm corn from California. And we have good burgers, Mama, good lean meat. I'll break yours up into pieces the way you like it. And see those," pointing to the bowl of fruit in the center of the table, "those are ripe peaches, Mama. You can't have any of those, but don't they look nice on the table?"

She turned to Peter with a radiant smile.

"She doesn't hear anything at all," she explained, "but still she likes the feeling of people talking to her."

Some little confabulation kept flaring up around the edges of the conversation, every time Lannie was asked to get up and go for anything for the table.

"Now stop that," Dr. Joe said finally, shaking his fork at the girl, "listen to your mama."

"Mama," Lannie said, "do you know what Harmony Mackleby said she would do if she had to put up with at home what I have to put up with?"

"Lana," said Beverly, smiling unperturbedly, "goes for her College Boards tomorrow. Now, Lannie's conscience tells her she can't go out last night with her friends, and out again tonight, and still do well on her exams. But still it rankles Lannie to hear these same sentiments spoken aloud by her parents," and she reached over and ran the back of her hand down Lannie's cheek.

A little later, apropos of something or other, Beverly said, "Oh, I'm sure our Lannie'll have a great success at that," and again reached over and rubbed her hand down Lannie's cheek, an old gesture, so familiar a gesture she seemed hardly aware of giving, or Lannie of receiving it.

"Success," Peter mused, "you know, I had my own little share of success once upon a time."

"Oh?"

"How come?"

"In fact"—and here he hesitated a moment—"I even had my picture on the cover of *Life* magazine one time."

"*Life*?"

"What d'you do?"

"Well—well, all right, I'll show you." He pushed back his chair and strode off to the other side, returning a minute later unrolling a giant sheet of poster paper.

It was a mockup of a *Life* cover for November 18, 1945, showing a crowd of women pushed against a chain-link fence, toward which a crowd of airmen was exuberantly racing. In the forefront of the picture, in a crooked aviator's cap, a small tearful boy stood holding a sign that read *Welcome Home Daddy I Missed You.*

"Have any of you seen this before?"

Lannie waved her hand in the air, "I have, I have, it's in our Crit Con book."

"Well, it's me." Holding the sheet up beside his face, Peter cocked his head and assumed a droll facsimile of that small boy's scowl. "It's me when I was four years old."

After the dishes had been cleared away, they brought their albums out to show him, and Dr. Joe got out his clarinet, which he claimed not to have touched in fifteen years, and played old band tunes from his touring days with the Royal Jesters, "Flirtation" and "Temptation" and "Talk to the Night," and Beverly and Lannie linked arms and bent their heads together and harmonized along, while Peter beat time with the tossers against the rim of the salad bowl, and even the old grandmother nodded along, her hand under the tablecloth, reading the beat off the tabletop with her fingertips.

A couple of nights after this, Peter ran into Lannie on the beach with two of her friends, a pair of chunky red-headed sisters with improbably long chins.

"Gretchen and Gloria Parisi, meet Mr. Peter Mikovich, alias Mickey."

The ocean was phosphorescent that night, streaks of blue phosphorescence folding over the edges of the waves, bright bubbles of phosphorescence popping all around their feet.

Peter said, "I just passed a girl with stripes painted across her forehead, two green stripes with a narrow blue stripe across the middle, do any of you know what that means?"

The two Parisi sisters looked at each other and smirked.

"Wichita Falls," the one said.

"Wichita Falls for sure."

Peter turned and continued down the beach.

"Hey?" Lannie called after him. "Are you going that way? Hey, wait a minute, I'll walk with you."

She ran to catch up, her feet kicking up sprays of phosphorescent sparks.

"It's paramecium," she told him, "millions on millions of tiny organisms, each with a tiny drop of phosphorus in its nucleus. Do you have any brothers or sisters?"

"I have two stepbrothers and a stepsister."

"I have one older brother named Denny. He's nineteen."

"I didn't know you have a brother."

"He doesn't come around too much. He and my papa do not get along. Are your stepbrothers and your stepsister on your one side or the other side?"

"My stepbrothers are on my mother's side, my stepsister's on my father's. As a matter of fact, until I was eighteen I didn't even know I had a stepsister."

He explained that after the divorce he hadn't seen much of his father, and for a long time hadn't even known he had remarried. He had been five at the time of the divorce, and only seven when his father died.

"After the war he'd started turning to drink. Actually, I don't remember him very well at all. But then when I was applying for college and wanted to take out Social Security, I went to see his second wife. It turns out she hadn't known about me, either. She was hugging me and crying. It seems I look a lot like him."

Lannie looked at him with sorry eyes and dragged her feet across the sand. She was wearing cutoffs and a sleeveless blouse, her hair pinned up underneath a triangular scarf, a key pinned to the pocket of her blouse with a safety pin. Her legs were long and still childishly thin, her back straight and pushed high, with sharply pronounced wings. She hugged herself and said, "You know, I'm terribly unhappy in my home life."

"Oh? I didn't know that."

"I haven't spoken to anyone about it. Oh, I tell my friends about it, but they don't understand. They understand how it feels, but not what it means."

"Would you like to talk about it now?"

"I have to tell someone. It's tearing me up inside."

They'd come to a promontory, a ragged rock tee stuck out into the surf, which Lannie mounted with half a dozen long, easy strides. By the time she'd reached the top, her heartache was all forgotten.

"My mama's had me taking ballet for six years now," she told Peter.

"And you don't like ballet?"

"No, I don't mind. It's good for legs and posture and it's true it does build character. But I always sweat a lot. We used to have a poodle named Buttons and he would always lick my face when I came in from practice. For the salt."

She was halfway turned, one arm raised with the fingertips resting on the tip of her collar, in a pose he imagined she'd picked out of some magazine or other. The waves hit straight against the face of the rock, and shot straight up into the air, forty, fifty yards over their heads, all around them a great roar and fall of water, though only the barest of sprays touched their skin. Spotlights were trained onto the promontory from the eaves of houses along the bluff, the water shimmering and silver in their glare. The light caught every peak and angle of her face, highlighting each tiny follicle and pore, and he could see her face essentially and as it would become in ten, in twenty years' time, at thirty, at forty-five, where the lines would begin to deepen, and the skin to fold—and then she turned, her braces sparkling, smiling the smile of a ten-year-old.

"How old would you be, Lannie? Sixteen?"

"Sixteen? Please, I'm seventeen. I'm going to be eighteen in two more months. My father was going to buy me a car for graduation, but I guess my mama's got him convinced to send me to Paris instead."

"And you'd rather have the car?"

"Well, I guess so."

This side was steeper. They descended backwards, she going ahead of him to point where he was to place his feet. It was another hundred yards to the steps to Chancery Lane, across a clear, level stretch of sand. This too was spotlighted, the light forming interlocking circles across the sand.

They walked from circle of light to circle of light, staggering and interweaving their tracks, while Peter recited for her the names of all the different dogs he'd ever owned, and how he used to feed grapefruits to the polar bears in the Highland Park zoo.

They dragged themselves up the steps panting and collapsing, in the manner of two people returning from a long and arduous trek. On the landing Lannie paused to empty out her shoes and brush the sand off the backs of her legs, supporting herself against his arm, and as she straightened up leaned up and took a swipe, no more than a taste really, from the corner of his mouth, then with a little dip and sidelong glance glided back—a small *développé* of provocation that he could see in another year or so becoming a ready part of her repertoire. A few minutes earlier he might have expected, while they were there on the rock had half expected, something like this, but now it took him completely off guard.

There was maybe another hundred yards to climb. Chancery was steep and winding along here, so steep and winding that at one point Peter tipped forward onto his hands.

Lannie laughed—her hand flying up to cover her braces.

He started clowning for her, jumped up onto a low

188

border wall and did a little tightrope walk across it, took a great leap down, and stubbed his toe, and went dancing all around on one foot.

Lannie laughed and laughed.

"That's like—that's like our Mr. Lee—"

"Mr. Lee, who he?"

"He's—he's—" but she was laughing too hard to get it out.

They separated and climbed to the deck by their respective stairs, arriving at the top at the same moment, on the exact same foot.

They pointed at each other and laughed.

Dr. Joe and Beverly were out. The lights on their side were out, except for a small lamp on the kitchen counter, and there was a note for Lannie on the door. Peter made as if to grab it—Lannie to crumple it up and swallow it.

They stood along the deck divider, shaking out the last little bits of their laughter

"Is your side the same size as ours?"

"No, actually it's much smaller. Just the living room and kitchen, and of course you can't count the bath. Want to see?"

He went in ahead of her, turning on all the lights. She entered on tiptoes, circling the whole way around the room and touching every piece of furniture before she would settle anywhere. He reached to pull the drapes—immediately she turned and darted out the door.

For a minute he thought he'd lost her. But then she returned with a hair brush and an opened can of cola, sat down on the daybed, and started unpinning her hair. She shook her head to one side and then the other, tugging at the brush, and tugging her head away from the brush. She was all seriousness now.

"Mr. Lee," she told him, "is our geometry teacher, Mr. Baskin Lee, born fifty-five years ago in Kanawha County, West Virginia—"

She told him about her teachers, which ones were fair, which ones she liked and didn't like, her friends, her locker, her words blending into one another fluid and melodic like a language you do not understand. She pinned her hair back up and refolded her scarf, carefully evening the edges and matching points, and tied it back on again, grooming her brush with her fingers and dropping the loose hair into an ash-tray on the coffee table, flipping as she talked through a copy of *Juris Doctor* that had been lying on the table. She'd missed a patch of sand just below her elbow, and each time she turned a page little granules of sand went skidding across the tabletop.

"Listen—do you know what happens when you break Ohm's Law?"

"Do I know what—"

"Aw, come on, you ought to know this one, you're a lawyer, aren't you? You have to go to the Circuit Court. That's what this dumb boy in my class said today. Do you think my mama's very pretty?"

"Very pretty," Peter agreed.

"She has pretty hands." Grimacing, Lannie held up her own stubby fingers and chewed-down nails. "Pugh!"

She jumped up and started for the door—wheeled around and grabbed her brush—and went on outside, arriving at the other side just as Beverly, in a white stole and evening gown, appeared at the top of the steps.

Lannie wrapped her arms around her, "Mama," and gave her a big hug, "Mama, did you have a lovely evening?"

Dr. Joe brought up the rear, carrying a huge horseshoe of yellow roses, which, spotting Peter at the door, he hoisted over his head.

"Second year in a row!"

Peter smiled and waved and stood a moment longer, surveying the night before turning in, and then turned off the deck lamp and closed the door.

190

He didn't see her on the deck the next afternoon when he came in from work, or in the living room that evening practicing her dancing, or hear her moving around the next morning as he usually did, getting ready for school while he was getting up for work—at which point he realized she was gone, realizing at the same moment how closely entwined his life was becoming with the life of the other side.

He judged from the tempo of footsteps crossing floors, of cupboard doors closing and water taps going on and off, that the mood next door was more one of anger than of alarm, her absence somehow tied in with some larger and apparently fairly populated circumstance. All weekend long their telephone rang, and he could hear Beverly's voice through the walls, quick, staccato bouts of words, punctuated with lengthy silences. All Friday evening and all day Saturday grim-faced couples kept appearing for little hubbubs with Beverly and Dr. Joe down at the bottom of the deck, sessions invariably ending with solemn handclasps and slow shakes of the head all around.

Shortly after dark on Saturday evening, Peter heard music out on the deck, and looking out saw Beverly standing alone at the railing, a glass in her hand. He made a trip down to the car, and on the way back remarked, "We haven't seen much of young Lannie these past couple days."

"Oh," scarcely turning her head to reply, "our Lannie's very much the independent young lady these days"—which was the extent of that.

A little while after that, though, as he was clearing off the table, he heard a commotion outside, and looking out saw Dr. Joe pulling a covered table onto the deck, with a blazing candelabra and a silver chafing dish, and a single white rosebud in a cut-glass vase.

Beverly paid him no mind.

He lifted the lid from the chafing dish, and a column of flame shot five feet into the air. Beverly was not impressed.

191

He went back inside, and came out wearing a wolf's mask, sniffing along the railing after her.

Beverly was not amused.

When Peter looked out again, though, they were both bent over their meal, and when he looked out a little later, they'd gone inside, or rather down to the end of the deck— just barely he could make out their outlines in the shadows around the picnic table.

As it happened, he had a good deal of work home with him that weekend. His work was an evening's ritual: each evening at seven, weekend and week night, he cleared the kitchen table and emptied out the contents of his case, items most pressing going across the front of the table, to be glanced over and thought about for a minute or two when he first sat down, and then moved to the back of the table to come back to later on, items upcoming and current fanning out in overlapping rows from either side of the case, those pending and merely germinating in topic-area piles across the back of the table, to be picked up and turned over in a stray minute here and there, each item as he finished with it going back into the case, and when everything was back in the case and the table was empty, then he was finished for the night, and each night he went through every item in his case. Next to his elbow lay three number 2 pencils, freshly sharpened; a Cordig 616 for signatures; a glass of plain tap water, that would sit beside him untouched the whole time he worked. All these were habits he'd picked up in the last, fitful months of his marriage, when every particular about the way he worked, down to the exact spot he set his glass, down to the precise order he pressed the snaps on his case, left before right, and closed them up again, right before left, was essential to him doing any work at all. He hadn't wanted the marriage to end, had battled against it every step of the way, on one occasion locking her inside their bedroom for two hours, on another slamming his fist into the garage door, breaking two bones.

He set fire to their safety deposit box, drove their new Caprice into the front of her parents' house in Storrs, doing over four thousand dollars' damage. Everything he did seemed only to strengthen her in her resolve.

At a certain point he'd reconciled himself, but still continued to act, partly out of pride, partly too out of what he came to see as a necessary process of shedding off. He saw he would have to give up everything, burn all bridges, raze the pastures, go away and leave nothing behind.

"If you'd only listened," she complained the last time they sat down together, "if only you'd accepted the fact."

But he had accepted the fact, earlier possibly than she would have imagined, and even as he was sitting here, raving and importuning, in some cool center of his brain he was only filing away details, her bracelet, the way she wore her hair, the color of her sweater, blue, a deep navy blue, that he wanted to be sure to remember.

At one point she got up and crossed the room, stopping for a moment with the window behind her and her head in silhouette—and he noted it. This was what he'd remember; this was what he'd take with him; this was what he had with him now, tilted back in his chair, his arms braced against the table's edge and head back, this was what he saw, the blue of her sweater, wave of her hair, her face in silhouette, images clean of any shadow of pain, or semblance of desire.

He worked through the better part of the next morning, too, but around noon restlessness began to overtake him, and around one he got up from the table, leaving everything lie, and went out for a drive.

He headed south on the Coast Highway, through Dana Point and San Juan-Capistrano, picking up the freeway at San Clemente and heading south.

It was a mild, clear, sunny day, the sort of bright California day that vivifies the skin, raising high crops of expectation in every fertile breast. To the right of him lay the ocean, sparkling under cloudless skies, to the left the coastline hills, yellow with wildflower, the air fragrant with wildflower, the highway jammed with cars, vans, busses, a stationwagon load of nuns with a ski rack on top, lone men driving with a wild determination, sixty-five, seventy-five, eighty miles an hour, bumpers never more than three, four feet apart. The lane to the left of him began to move, twenty yards, thirty yards, forty yards forward, and held there for a moment, and then began to ease back, almost to the same spot back, and the line on the other side started to move, thirty yards, forty yards forward, and held there for a moment, and then began to ease back, and his own line started to move, twenty yards, thirty yards, and each time the faces went by each other, a look would go back and forth, a smiling recognition. He got where he could tell which would be the next car to switch a lane. All the cars were switching lanes, never more than one at any given time, but always one, and immediately after it another one. He was switching, too, over the left a lane, and then one more, and then back one, and that lane started to move, twenty, thirty, forty yards, the steering wheel blending into his hands, the gas pedal to his foot, the miles slipping effortlessly under him, mile by mile by mile.

That feeling lasted almost into San Diego, but on the outskirts of San Diego the traffic started thickening up, and at each intersection there were cars and more cars, until he turned off, finally, at one of the La Jolla exits, and started back.

It was dusk by the time he reached home, and as he climbed the steps to the deck he discovered Lannie was back, in cutoffs and a blue T-shirt that read Kiss Me Quick I'm Melting In The Sun, arguing with her mother.

"And then—"

"What was I supposed to, I'm supposed to—"

"—to think you can stand there and—"

Spotting Peter, Beverly, with a little downward jerk of

exasperation, turned and stalked off into the house. But Lannie was irrepressible, rearing up on tiptoes, waving excitedly.

"Mickey, I'm, hi, I'm home from La Jolla!"

The coincidence of La Jolla set him back for a moment.

"Well—and how was La Jolla?"

"It was trig, that's the word they have down there, Mickey, it was trig, it was great!"

At first though it'd been ugly. There were twenty-six of them and they weren't telling anyone where they were going but were just leaving notes. They were going into the desert rock climbing except when they got to Lake Elsinore she and Harmony decided they'd go to La Jolla instead. The first two nights they stayed with Harmony's sister Madge, and it was ugly, Madge's boyfriend was a junkie, he'd been surfing semifinalist in 1972, but now when they woke up he'd taken Harmony's expensive wristwatch and her own hairdryer and they went out walking and couldn't get in any bars and finally were just sitting on the curb looking at the beach and eating tacos and trying to decide whether to go to the zoo or take a bus to Tijuana when James came by walking two dogs named Phideaux with a Ph and a deaux and Bowser and offered they could at least come over to his place for something to eat and stay if they liked. That's when she met Dan and Don who were identical twins except she could tell them apart from the start and their cousin Jan Arrow who did leatherwork from Portland. And that night while she was trying to sleep in the chair and couldn't get to sleep that way, she went over to the big waterbed where they were all sleeping and Dan was awake and made room for her and stayed up all night talking to her and didn't try anything, even lay with his arms under him so she'd have room. Bowser and Phideaux were Dan's dogs, James had just been walking them. And she didn't think too much about it until he started meeting her on the beach and taking her into bars and he took her out to dinner and even bought her a hairdryer for the one T. J. Riddle, that was Madge's boyfriend's name, T. J. Riddle had taken. And while they were sitting in the bar James got up on the stool beside her and said, Look, you know Dan's folks have lots of money, they own lots of Calgon and have two miles of beachfront in Santa Barbara, and then she'd been glad, glad they'd picked each other first without that.

"And he's going to find us a place and send me bus fare to come down there anytime I want to, and he's going to drive up here and meet Mama—"

"Lana," just then Beverly appeared at the screendoor, "I wonder would you come inside here a minute, please, there's something more I'd like to say to you."

Lannie rolled her eyes and whispered, "She says I'm not ever to go down there again, but what she doesn't know is I'm already gone," and skipped on inside.

Peter went inside and washed his face, cleared the table off and put his case away in the closet and was pulling the drapes, just letting go of the cord, when he was hit by a feeling, very like remorse, that started at the knees and moved up fast.

He sat down on the daybed, lay back, laced his hands behind his neck. It was a large and fairly complicated feeling, and in order to deal with it at all he had to break it down into pieces and deal with each piece individually, taking each one up and turning it over in his mind and looking it over from every angle, and then putting it aside. Some of these pieces seemed to be of a larger component, which on closer inspection turned out only to have been the stray accumulation, the random configuration of the debris of an active life. Some of these, too, came back to him in new guises—and again he took them up and turned them over in his mind, viewing them from every side, and put them aside, and each time they came back a little diminished, a little less insistently, until none of them came back again, and all of the feeling was gone.

He ran a short check then for accountability, anywhere he might have done anything he might not otherwise have done, anywhere he might have misrepresented his intentions or himself.

After a certain point in the evening the ocean sound became distinguishable above the traffic sounds farther down the hill. For a while he'd been able to hear them arguing on the other side, their voices tugging back and forth, and then for a long time now there'd been nothing. Possibly he slept a while, because the next that he heard was music playing on the deck, and he got up and went to the door to look.

At first he could see nothing, and was about to go back inside when he saw a flash of white, and then another in the shadows underneath the sunscreen. It was Beverly, dancing by herself at the other end of the deck.

She moved slowly, absentmindedly, her head bent, the slack of her skirt gathered up between two fingers. She turned, pushed up onto her toes, and lifted one leg slowly out behind her. She turned, and as she turned caught sight of Peter standing at the door. For a moment she hesitated— and then drifted back down to the end of the deck, swaying there in the shadows for a minute, and then slowly began to transcribe a circle around the edge of the deck, and as she made the turn, again her eyes met his, with a look that was challenging and provocative, inviting and promising, and at the same time none of these, and she turned, skimming the surface of the deck with short mountings of the foot that barely lifted the level of her shoulders, her head pivoting against the sway of her body, and she turned, dipped, stepped, and turned, in slow, measured counterpoint to the music.